Nim at Sea

Wendy Orr

Illustrated by Kerry Millard

PUFFIN

PUFFIN BOOKS

Published by the Penguin Group
Penguin Books Ltd, 80 Strand, London WC2R ORL, England
Penguin Group (USA) Inc., 375 Hudson Street, New York, New York 10014, USA
Penguin Group (Canada), 90 Eglinton Avenue East, Suite 700, Toronto, Ontario, Canada M4P 2Y3
(a division of Pearson Penguin Canada Inc.)
Penguin Ireland, 25 St Stephen's Green, Dublin 2, Ireland (a division of Penguin Books Ltd)
Penguin Group (Australia), 250 Camberwell Road, Camberwell, Victoria 3124, Australia
(a division of Pearson Australia Group Pty Ltd)
Penguin Books India Pvt Ltd, 11 Community Centre, Panchsheel Park, New Delhi – 110 017, India
Penguin Group (NZ), 67 Apollo Drive, Rosedale, North Shore 0632, New Zealand
(a division of Pearson New Zealand Ltd)
Penguin Books (South Africa) (Pty) Ltd, 24 Sturdee Avenue, Rosebank,
Johannesburg 2196, South Africa

Penguin Books Ltd, Registered Offices: 80 Strand, London WC2R ORL, England

puffinbooks.com

First published in Australia by Allen & Unwin 2007
First published in Great Britain in Puffin Books 2008
1

Set in Minion
Made and printed in England by Clays Ltd, St Ives plc

British Library Cataloguing in Publication Data
A CIP catalogue record for this book is available from the British Library

ISBN: 978-0-141-32409-8

For Paula, who believed in Nim W. O.

For Wendy, and all of the stories we've shared K. M.

LONG AGO, when Nim was a baby, she'd had both a mother and a dad. Then one day, her mother had decided to investigate the contents of a blue whale's stomach. It was an interesting experiment that no one had done for thousands of years, and Nim's dad, Jack, said that it would have been all right, it should have been safe – but the Troppo Tourists came to make a film of it, shouting and racing their huge pink-and-purple boat round Nim's mother and the whale. The whale panicked and dived, so deep that no one ever knew where or when he came back up again.

Nim's mother never came back up at all.

So Jack packed his baby onto his boat and sailed round and round the world – and finally, when the baby had grown into a very little girl, he found the perfect island where he could do his science and Nim could grow, wild and free like the animals they lived with.

The island had white shell beaches, pale-gold sand and tumbled black rocks. It had a fiery mountain with green rainforest on the high slopes and grasslands at the bottom.

There was a pool of fresh water to drink, a waterfall to slide down and a hidden hollow where the grasslands met the beach. That's where Jack built their hut.

Best of all there was a maze of reef guarding the island from everything but the smallest boats, because Jack and Nim didn't want the Troppo Tourists or anyone else to find their island. But one day, Jack and his boat got lost in a storm – and Nim's email friend, Alex Rover, the most famous and cowardly adventure writer in the whole world, came to rescue Nim.

And then Nim's most secret wish came true: Jack came floating back and Alex stayed.

1

IN A PALM TREE, on an island, in the middle of the wide blue sea, was a girl.

Nim's hair was wild, her eyes were bright, and round her neck she wore three cords. One was for a spyglass, one for a whirly, whistling shell and the other a fat red, pocketknife in a sheath.

With the spyglass at her eye, Nim watched the little red seaplane depart. It sailed out through the reef to the deeper dark ocean, bumping across the waves till it was tossed into the bright blue sky. Then it rose so high and so far it was nothing but a speck, and floated out of sight.

'Alex is gone,' Nim told Fred.

Fred stared at the coconuts clustered on the trunk.

Fred was an iguana, spiky as a dragon, with a cheerful snub nose. He was sitting on Nim's shoulder, but he cared more about coconuts than he did about saying goodbye. (Marine iguanas don't eat coconut, but no one had ever told Fred.)

As Nim threw three ripe coconuts *thump* into the sand, she remembered Alex saying, 'I never knew anything could taste better than coffee!' the first time Nim opened a coconut for her.

Nim looked down at her father, sitting like a stone on Selkie's Rock. Jack's head was bowed and his shoulders slumped. Nim had never seen him look so alone.

And she knew she'd made a terrible, terrible mistake, worse than anything she'd ever done before.

THE FIRST MISTAKE was when she answered Alex's very first email, back when she'd thought that the famous Alex Rover was a man and a Hero like the hero in his books. That had been a good mistake, because when Alex ended up on the island, Jack and Nim wanted her never to leave. Sometimes it felt good to be three instead of two.

But other times Nim wanted Jack just for herself, the way it used to be, and sometimes she wanted Alex just for herself, because Alex was *her* friend before she was Jack's. Sometimes, when Alex and Jack told Nim to go to sleep while they talked late in the night, Nim felt left out and more lonely than she'd ever been when they were two.

And then, this morning, the little red seaplane had arrived with all the things that Alex had asked her editor in the city to send. It was the first time a plane had ever landed on Nim's island. Nim could see Jack was worried that the pilot would notice how beautiful the island was and would want to come back again and again.

Whenever Jack was worried, Nim was too. And when Nim was worried, so were Selkie and Fred. (Selkie was a sea lion, and sometimes she forgot that Nim was a girl and not a little sea lion pup to be looked after and whuffled over.) They both stuck close to Nim every time she walked back and forth from the plane to the hut.

'I've never seen animals do that before!' exclaimed the pilot.

Nim didn't know what to say, partly because she didn't know exactly what he hadn't seen before, and partly because she'd never spoken to anyone except Jack and Alex. She grabbed a crate and opened it up. Inside there were books. Thin books and fat, short books and tall, history books and science, mysteries and fairy tales. Nim didn't know what to read first.

'Come on,' said Alex. 'There'll be time to read when everything's off the plane.'

The pilot pulled out two big solar panels. 'Great!' Jack exclaimed, because he wanted them for the new room he planned to add – one especially for Alex to write her books. Jack balanced the panels on his head and walked very slowly and carefully up to the hut.

'Who's going to take this one?' the pilot asked, pointing to a crate. Nim stepped forward. But just as she was about to reach for the crate, the pilot handed it to Alex. First Alex stumbled, then she tripped, then *crash!* the crate fell to the sand with a tinkle of broken glass.

'Oh, *no*!' Alex wailed. 'What have I done?'

'Jack's test tubes!' Nim shouted. 'You should have let me take it!'

'I was trying to help!'

'But I didn't need help! You just got in the way!'

'I'm always in the way,' Alex snapped. 'Maybe you and Jack would be better off without me.'

'Maybe we would!' Nim shouted and stomped off without waiting for an answer.

She's right! Alex thought. Nim and Jack lived here perfectly happily all those years without anyone else – they don't really need me. Nim's been cross with me a lot lately and I've never seen Jack so worried. I think . . . I think I'm changing their lives too much. What if they've secretly been wanting their old lives back – and are too nice to say so?

Alex understood about being afraid to say so. Before she came to the island, she was so afraid of saying anything to anyone that she'd hardly ever left her apartment. She was famous, but only through her books. Her life had changed completely since she flew across the world to find Nim.

'Last one!' The pilot handed her a large envelope. 'And, now, time for me to go.'

Alex opened it and pulled out a letter. 'Wait! Can I . . . can I go with you?'

'Sure!' he said. 'But don't you need to pack anything?'

Alex knew that if she saw Jack or Nim, she would never be able to leave, even if it was the right thing to do. 'No,' she said, 'I'm ready to go.'

She climbed into the little red seaplane. And was gone.

NIM SCRAMBLED DOWN from the coconut palm and buried her face in Selkie's warm neck, because the sea lion loved her no matter how bad Nim was – and the feeling in Nim's stomach told her this was the very worst thing she'd ever done.

Jack loved her too, but Nim didn't know if he still would when he realized it was Nim who had chased Alex away.

'Meet me at the Emergency Cave,' she told Selkie, because suddenly the sun and sea were much too bright. Only the deepest, darkest cave could match the way she felt inside.

Selkie gave a disapproving sort of *hrumph* and lolloped down to the sea. Nim and Fred headed inland, towards the bottom of Fire Mountain, past the Hissing Stones and across the Black Rocks.

Scrambling up the boulders was good, because it was such hard work Nim couldn't think about anything else.

Emergency
Cave

Fire Mountain

Winds

Rainforest

Pool

Tabletop
Garden

Frigate Bird
Cliffs

But when she got to the cave, she remembered: Alex telling her stories when they were trying to sleep on the hard cave floor, Alex watching the sun rise on the very first morning, Alex crying when Nim skinned her knee.

Nim crawled into the deepest corner of the cave to be as alone as she could possibly be. She hiccuped and coughed and cried and blew her nose, and dropped her hanky.

When she was feeling around in the dark for her soggy hanky, she found a map.

It was the map Alex had drawn when she told one of her stories: a map of an island that was a city with an even bigger city on the land behind. It was as different from Nim's island as anywhere could be.

That's where Alex's books were published, in a tall, shining building whose top floors were up above the clouds. That's where Alex's editor was – the one who'd sent the supply plane that Alex had just left on.

Nim stuffed the map into her deepest pocket and started crying all over again. She cried so hard that Selkie pulled herself all the way up from the sea to the cave to comfort her. But when Nim wouldn't stop crying, no matter how much Selkie whuffled and snuffled, Selkie went outside to do tricks to make her laugh. She balanced a rock on her nose, threw it up in the air and off the cliff. She sat up high on her tail and flapped her flippers as if she were trying to fly. She did a handstand on her front flippers. She went through all her tricks over and over and barked at Nim in between to make her stop crying.

Finally, Selkie produced her best trick ever – a handstand right on the edge of the rocks, then a flip into a perfect dive all the way down to the water.

It was a long way down and it was a very good trick – but Nim didn't come out to see.

And so Nim also didn't see the giant cruise ship that had come round the point and anchored not far from the cliffs.

She didn't see the inflatable motorboat with people snorkelling around it, or the second motorboat chugging quietly out from the other side of the ship. She didn't see the man watching Selkie do her tricks through his binoculars, lift his rifle and shoot Selkie with a tranquillizer dart.

She didn't see him instruct his crew to heave Selkie into his boat and speed away with her to their ship.

BUT FRED DID.

Fred had been watching Selkie and hoping she'd do his favourite flipping-a-coconut-high-off-the-cliffs-*smash!*-onto-the-rocks trick. When she did the handstand-dive, he ran to the edge of the cliff to see if she'd smashed a coconut on her way down.

What he saw made Fred forget all about coconuts.

First he scrambled down, then he scrambled back up. Then he rushed into the cave and headbutted Nim's leg. When she still didn't pay attention, he climbed onto her shoulder and sneezed his cool saltwater spray in her face.

'Yuck, Fred!' said Nim, but when Fred scurried to the edge of the cliff, Nim followed.

The boat was heading back to the ship. Through her spyglass Nim could see Selkie at the bottom of the boat.

'They've killed her!' Nim screamed.

But then Selkie lifted her head, and Nim saw the men tying ropes and nets round her.

She had to save her friend. Fast!

Fred scrambled to her shoulder and clung on tight. Nim stood on the edge of the cliff. The water was a long way down.

What if I hit the rocks? Nim thought.

She jumped, as high and far as she could, and twisted into a dive.

She hit the water.

Nim's lungs were bursting and her ears were hurting. Then she saw the light above her head, and kicked and spluttered her way up to the air.

The boat was already a long way out, and the waves were strong on this side of the island, but Nim had no choice. She took another deep breath and began to swim.

JACK SAT ON Selkie's Rock for a long, long time, staring out at the empty sky. He felt as if half his world had gone up with Alex's plane and that he'd been left behind.

He reread the letter he'd found on the beach: the letter she'd left for him to find.

Dear Alex,

I'm glad the materials I organized for the supply ship were useful; I hope these things will all be too. I guess that new cabin must be just about finished by now and you've all got clothes to wear again. It was quite amusing to read about your banana-leaf dress in your first email!

Your apartment and furniture have been sold, as you instructed. I'm enclosing all the paperwork. However, just in case you change your mind about staying on that little island forever, I'm also enclosing your new passport and credit card to replace the ones you lost.

Now please find enclosed the reason I've been so busy: the first copy of your new book. I am very proud to be the editor of

this book: I think it's wonderful and we're going all out to make
sure it'll be your best-seller ever.

Please let me know if there's anything else I can do.
Yours,
Delia Defoe

'Why would she . . . ?' said Jack. But no matter how many times he read the letter, it still didn't explain why Alex had gone.

'Could she have changed her mind about selling her apartment?' he asked the sea. 'Did she suddenly want to go and be famous? And why couldn't she tell me?'

But the sea didn't answer, and it didn't matter what Jack wondered, because Alex was gone – and soon he'd have to tell Nim, which would be almost worse than knowing it himself.

Jack was certain he knew exactly where Nim was. He'd seen her face when she'd opened that big crate of books: she'd be lying somewhere, her head on Selkie's back and Fred curled on her stomach, lost in a story, not even realizing that everything had changed.

ALEX SAT IN the passenger seat of the seaplane, too frozen with sadness to even be afraid. She looked back at the gold sand of Turtle Beach, the black Sea Lion Rocks, the palm tree Nim always climbed and the shack they'd just built, and she wondered if she was making a terrible mistake.

Then she thought about what Nim had said and knew she cared too much about her friends to stay if Nim didn't want her.

FRED JUMPED OFF Nim's shoulder when they hit the water, but he only stayed under long enough to grab one big mouthful of seaweed before popping out beside her.

Selkie was part of Fred's life and Fred wanted her back.

They were both swimming as fast as they could, straight out to sea, but the boat was pulling away faster. Nim's heart was pounding; it hurt when she breathed and she was swallowing water faster than she could spit it out.

I . . . *huff* . . . can't . . . go . . . *huff* . . . fast enough! she thought. She rolled onto her back. Fred kept on gliding under the water just beside her.

When Nim had caught her breath and rolled over again, the cruise ship was getting closer – but the motorboat with Selkie and the seal-nappers had disappeared.

It can't have gone! Nim thought. It must be on the other side of the ship.

That was when she saw the huge pink-and-purple name on the ship's bow: TROPPO TOURIST.

The company that Nim and Jack hated more than anything in the world.

Nim tried to swim faster, but it didn't take long before she was gasping and swallowing water again. She rolled on her back again; her arms whirred, her legs kicked . . . and her head knocked hard against a rubber boat.

Hands grabbed her arms. A man and a woman, with horrified faces and matching pink-and-purple T-shirts, stared down at her.

'Fred!' screamed Nim.

Fred scrabbled to her shoulder and they were hauled into an inflatable motorboat like the one that had seal-napped Selkie.

'You said you'd counted!' shouted the woman whose T-shirt said *I'm Kylie*.

'I did!' the man named Kelvin answered. 'There were fifteen kids in that snorkelling group and we took fifteen back. I think.'

'If you'd counted,' Kylie insisted, 'we wouldn't be fishing this poor kid out of the water just before the ship is set to sail!'

'Maybe she's a castaway from that deserted island. We've found Kid Crusoe!'

'You're not funny,' Kylie snapped.

Nim didn't have enough breath to say her name was Nim Rusoe, not Kid Crusoe.

'Where were you heading to, kid?'

'To the boat,' Nim whispered.

She still couldn't see the other little boat. All she could see was the cruise ship: its white length stretching forever in front of her and its towering decks reaching to the sky.

It was the only place Selkie's boat could have come from and the only place it could have gone. If Nim was going to rescue Selkie, she had to get on this ship.

Fred sneezed.

'What *is* that?' Kelvin demanded.

'I don't care what it is – throw it back!'

Fred clung tight to Nim and glared his fiercest dragon glare. 'He's my friend!' Nim shouted.

'If you say so,' Kelvin grinned. He didn't look as if he really wanted to touch Fred anyway.

'She's delirious.'

'We'd better let her keep it.'

'Where's your snorkel, honey?'

'I don't know,' said Nim.

'Never mind,' said Kylie, with a big phoney smile. 'We won't tell anyone you lost a valuable snorkel if you don't tell anyone you nearly missed the boat.'

'Great idea!' said Kelvin. 'Look, kid, we don't want to get you into trouble. Your parents would be pretty mad if they found out you hadn't stayed with the other kids the way you were supposed to.'

'You'd probably be grounded all the way to New York City!'

'Stuck in your cabin for six whole days – you wouldn't like that, would you?'

Nim felt as if her head was going to explode. 'Where's *Selkie*?' she shouted.

'Who's Selkie?'

'We haven't lost another kid, have we?'

'She's a . . .' But Nim stopped just before she said 'sea lion'. She remembered the part in Alex's book when the Hero tricked the Bad Guys out of kidnapping him, because they thought he was crazy.

'. . . a mermaid,' said Nim.

'She's had too much sun!'

'Too long in the water!'

'Wrap her up – grab that jacket.'

Kelvin dropped a pink-and-purple Troppo jacket over Nim and Fred. He still didn't seem to want to touch Fred.

Kylie looked at him the way Selkie glared at Fred when he ate Nim's lunch. 'Don't worry, kiddo, I'll get you settled down before you see your parents; you'll be fine!'

The boat bumped against the ship. A long plank with rope railings led up from the water to a door halfway along the side. Kelvin grabbed a rope, and Kylie pushed Nim up the ramp and onto the ship.

3

NIM WAS IN a big, open room with small palm trees and large, bright flowers. There were decks above her, a long hall lined with doors leading off to the left and a white stone fountain to the right. And everywhere she looked there were people: sitting on the edge of the fountain, looking out over the rail, relaxing in deck chairs, perched at small tables with drinks and snacks, sitting at desks across from beaming Troppo Tourist crew members. They were talking and laughing and smiling and scowling and gazing around.

Nim froze.

'Are you okay?' Kylie asked sharply.

Nim nodded, but she could hardly breathe. She took a step closer to the fountain where water bubbled and splashed from the mouth of a carved stone dolphin. In the tiny pool around it were two dolphins swimming in endless circles.

Nim gasped. The dolphins she knew swam free and far across the sea – but these animals barely had room to splash.

'This way,' Kylie said, quickly steering Nim down a flight of stairs and into another long hallway with a shiny green floor and walls lined with doors. There were no windows, and even though light shone from bright lamps in the ceiling, Nim felt as closed-in as if she were in a cave. Fred curled himself tightly round her neck, peering out from under her chin.

Kylie pulled out a key, unlocked the door marked 12 and pushed Nim into a cabin. There were two bunk beds, two sets of drawers and a door into a tiny, shiny room. She reached in and handed Nim a towel.

'You'd better get warm and dry before you go back to the Kids' Klub,' she said. 'Were you supposed to have lunch with your mum and dad?'

'No,' said Nim.

'Well, how about I get you something yummy? What about a hamburger and milkshake? A bit of lunch and you'll feel all better.'

'I don't know,' said Nim.

Kylie's smile got even bigger and phonier. 'You'll be fine, you'll see!' She stepped out of the door, called, 'Have a shower if you want; that'll warm you up!' and disappeared.

Fred crawled down from Nim's shoulder. Nim waited a second and tried to open the door.

The door wouldn't open.

Nim had lived all her life on the island. She'd read about locks, but she'd never seen one. She'd never known what it would be like to be inside a small room and not be able to get out. She pulled the knob and kicked the door as hard as she could.

'Ow!' she shouted, rubbing her big toe.

'Now what do we do?' she asked Fred.

Fred felt braver now that Kylie was gone. He decided to explore the cabin. In the tiny room behind the door he'd found an even tinier room with glass walls and a hard floor with a hole in the middle.

Alex had told Nim about toilets that flushed and showers like waterfalls that ran as hot or as cold as you liked. When Nim wanted to get clean, she swam in the sea or soaked in the rainforest pool. But now she turned the tap on – and the water gushed out just like Alex said, warm as sunshine.

'I'll try it if you will!' she told Fred.

Nim stuck her arm under the spray, then her leg and then she and Fred jumped back and forth under the water and out of the door, till there were puddles on the floor, splashes up the walls and drops on the ceiling. Fred got so hot he couldn't stay still and raced crazily around the cabin and up and down the bunks till he was worn out. Nim turned the tap off, rubbed her hair with the towel and shook herself to dry her clothes.

She was wearing the blue shirt and red trousers made with the material from the supply ship. Jack had designed the trousers with drawstring legs that could be pushed up into shorts for coolness or pulled down smooth for swimming or palm-tree-climbing. There were lots of pockets for Useful Things, including one extra deep pocket with its own drawstring to keep special things safe. Nim pushed the legs up into shorts now, because they were soggy and dripping.

Everything else in the bathroom was soggy too and quite a lot of things in the cabin – especially the pillow Fred was stretched out on.

The door opened and Kylie came in with a tray piled with food. Her face went pale when she saw the cabin. 'I see you had a shower!' she exclaimed with a forced little laugh. 'I bet you feel better now!'

'A little bit,' Nim said.

'Well, this ought to fix it. Look what I've brought you: milkshake, hamburger, chips, some jelly and cake and banana for dessert, and a hot chocolate in case you're still cold.'

'Thank you,' said Nim. She stared at the food and

wondered what to try first: the banana was the only thing she recognized. She put it in her pocket when Kylie wasn't looking.

'Those are interesting shorts you're wearing,' Kylie said. 'I thought they were a wetsuit.'

'They're wet shorts,' Nim explained. She opened the hamburger and found some lettuce. Something else I know! Nim thought, but Fred snatched it and gulped it down. She'd have to try the strange foods.

The milkshake slid cold down her throat and then hot chocolate warmed it up again. Nim tried a mouthful of slippery green jelly. She liked the way it squished through her teeth. She ate a handful of hot, salty chips and the pickle from the hamburger. Fred did too. Fred liked the jelly best. Nim liked the hot chocolate. And the salty chips. It was hard to decide.

Kylie watched Nim and Fred trying the food, mouthful by mouthful. 'That's an interesting way to eat,' she said.

'It's interesting food,' Nim said politely.

Suddenly there was a faint rumble from somewhere deep inside the ship and the floor beneath Nim's bare feet began a steady, chugging tremble. The ship's engines had started.

If I don't get out of here, thought Nim, it'll be too late!

'Do you feel well enough to go back to the Kids' Klub?'

Nim nodded. She had to start looking for Selkie somewhere.

'Do you want to take that – I mean, your friend – with you?'

Fred rushed to the plate, slurped down the last of the jelly and raced up to Nim's shoulder. Nim picked up the pink-and-purple jacket. She thought a disguise might be useful. She threw the jacket over Fred on her shoulder so he was disguised too, all except for his watching eyes and iguana grin.

They followed Kylie down the hall to a fish tank with a sign that said PIRANHA DECK. Nim held Fred's tail to make extra sure he didn't fall in.

Kylie stopped and pressed a button on the wall opposite the tank. Doors slid open and she ushered Nim and Fred into a small, empty room. All that was in it was a doormat that said THURSDAY, a mirror on the wall to see their own frightened faces and a row of buttons beside the door with a picture of an animal on each one. Kylie pressed the ARMADILLO button and the doors slid shut.

Nim knew about elevators: Alex had told her about her home, an apartment building that was half as high as Fire Mountain, with elevators that took her up and down if she ever wanted to go out. What Nim didn't know was that the elevator would leave her stomach down at the bottom while it whisked the rest of her up to the top. Fred didn't know either. He was so surprised he sneezed his last mouthful of jelly all over Nim's neck.

'Yuck, Fred!' said Nim. It was the first completely true thing she'd said since she'd got on the ship.

'I bet your friends will be glad to see you,' Kylie said as the elevator stopped.

The only friends Nim had ever had were Selkie and Fred, plus Chica the sea turtle and Galileo the frigate bird – but Chica only came ashore once a year to lay her eggs and Galileo was only your friend if you had a fish in your hand. So for just a minute Nim thought, Selkie's here!

But when the elevator doors opened, the sign said ARMADILLO DECK and the cage beneath it held two little armadillos rolled into tight, armour-plated balls.

Kylie turned and Nim followed her towards a swimming pool. Selkie wasn't in it or in the little pool behind it with spray that fountained up like water through the rocks of her own Keyhole Cove. They walked on, past a door marked TROPPO TEENS, past another marked TROPPO TOTS and opened the KIDS' KLUB door.

Inside, people were making things at tables, others were playing games on giant computer screens, some were running and others were talking; some were bigger than Nim and some smaller. They were as crowded and noisy as seagulls on a beach – and, except for another Troppo Tourist woman whose pink-and-purple T-shirt said *Kristie*, they were all . . .

. . . Kids! Nim thought. I didn't think there'd be this many kids in a whole city!

Kylie pushed her firmly into the room and pulled Kristie out of the door. 'Not quite right in the head,' Nim heard her say. 'She shouldn't have been allowed to go snorkelling – and look at the lizard she caught out there! We couldn't get it away from her.'

'Never mind – the Professor can deal with that.'

Nim wasn't listening.

In the books Nim had read, kids had adventures together; sometimes they were friends at the beginning of the story and other times they fought and ended up friends in the end. But how are you supposed to know what to do, Nim wondered, when you can't even figure out what they're doing – and they don't even notice you?

She backed against the wall and watched them as if they were a flock of birds that weren't used to her yet.

A girl in front of one of the giant computer screens stopped spinning her steering wheel and looked right at

Nim. She smiled and Nim tried to smile back. The girl came over.

'I'm Erin. Did you get on at that port two days ago too? I thought we were the only ones.' She pointed to a slightly smaller dark-haired boy who was riding a strange sort of motorbike that kept bouncing him off the seat but didn't go anywhere. 'That's Ben.'

Fred stuck his head out from under the jacket and sneezed.

'Cool!' said Erin. 'What's his name?'

Suddenly a bunch of kids were round them, so close Nim could hardly breathe, asking questions so fast no one even noticed she wasn't answering.

'Where'd you get that thing?'

'Can I touch it?'

'What *is* it?'

'How come the Professor let you have it?'

Fred sneezed again, harder, and they jumped back.

Kristie came back inside and the kids turned to her.

'Look what the Professor gave her!'

'Of course!' Kristie exclaimed. 'You must be the Professor's kid!'

Nim didn't know what a Professor's kid was, but she knew that it might be the disguise that would let her save Selkie.

'All right then, why don't you tell us about your little friend here?'

'He's a marine iguana,' Nim began. 'He can swim and dive …'

'Does he do tricks?'

'Show us some tricks!'

Nim thought fast. Fred could do lots of things. He could gulp down coconut so fast he wouldn't even notice a pearl inside. He could play coconut football. He could sink like a stone to the bottom of Keyhole Cove. He could ride on Nim's shoulder and sneeze on her neck.

'Ladies and Gentlemen!' she began, imitating Alex's best storytelling voice, 'Allow me to present: *Fred*!'

Fred stuck his head out from behind her neck to see why she was calling him, saw all the people staring and stared back even harder.

It wasn't exactly a trick, but: 'Fred here is a champion starer,' said Nim. 'He can stare hard enough to make anyone look away!'

'Not me!' said a red-haired boy. He came closer and stared into Fred's eyes. Fred stared back. The boy moved closer. Fred sneezed.

'Gross!' shouted the boy and jumped back into the crowd.

Everyone laughed and clapped.

'Thank you, Fred!' said Nim. 'What would you like to do for your next trick?'

Fred stared at her. His mouth opened and shut as if he was eating.

'I don't have any coconut,' said Nim.

Fred brought his face right up to hers and stared harder.

Everyone laughed again. 'Does he really understand?' asked a girl in a sunflower hat.

'No,' said Kristie. 'I went to the Professor's lecture on reptiles and he said they don't understand language.'

'Is he really hungry?' Erin asked Nim.

'Fred's always hungry,' said Nim.

Erin reached for a plate of fruit on a table and held out a segment of mandarin. Fred snatched, started to gulp – and spat mashed mandarin across the room.

Kids jumped, yelled and laughed. All except Erin and Ben, who'd finally got off the jolting motorbike and was watching quietly.

'I'm sorry, Fred!' Erin said and gave him a kiwi fruit. Fred didn't like kiwi fruit either. Chomps of green mush flew across the room and everyone laughed harder. Erin looked as if she was going to cry.

'He likes strawberries,' said Nim.

Erin grabbed a strawberry, Fred gulped it down – and didn't spit it out.

Everyone clapped.

'Fred has lots of other tricks,' said Nim, 'but he mostly does them with another performer. He needs to go and rehearse with her now.'

Fred settled himself back on her shoulder and Nim marched out of the door.

Oh, Selkie! she thought. Where are you?

JACK STILL HADN'T moved. He still couldn't believe that Alex had gone and still couldn't figure out what to say to Nim. 'Let her be happy a little longer,' he decided and went on staring out at the empty sea.

ALEX WAS STILL frozen in her seat, clutching the envelope the pilot had handed her just before she'd jumped on board.

She knew it held the first copy of her new book and she wasn't ready to see it yet. There was also a credit card, passport and a thick contract saying that her apartment and furniture had been sold. She'd asked Delia to do that, but she was surprised that there was no letter explaining it.

Just as she remembered that there *had* been a letter and realized she must have dropped it as she climbed on board, the little red seaplane bumped gently down onto the waves and pulled up beside the Sunshine Island wharf. Alex wiped her eyes and climbed out.

It was three months since she'd landed here on her way to find Nim. She'd been nervous then, afraid of flying, afraid of crowds, afraid of the sea – yet it had been exciting too, because she'd been turning into someone new. But if Nim didn't want her on the island any more, there was nothing to do but go home.

Except that, according to the contract she'd just read, she didn't have a home.

'You have to go somewhere!' she told herself.

'Can you take me to the airport on Isla Grande when you've refuelled?' she asked the pilot. He shook his head.

'I'm afraid my old plane needs more than fuel after such a long flight. She'll have to be completely serviced before I take her anywhere else.'

'How about when you're finished?'

'It'll be too dark,' the pilot said. 'I'm not an adventurer like you, Alex Rover! The Sunshine Island Seaplane and I don't fly at night.'

'Okay,' said Alex. 'I guess I'll have to find the pilot who flew me here from the big island before.' She took a bus to the little airport.

'Sorry, miss,' the man in the terminal office said. 'The Thursday flight to Isla Grande left half an hour ago. We won't be going again till Tuesday.'

'Five days!' Alex exclaimed. 'I can't wait that long!'

'Well, there's a cruise ship coming in this afternoon.'

'I'll take it,' said Alex.

'It's going all the way to New York City if you like.'

'I'd like,' said Alex.

As the man processed her ticket, Alex looked around the terminal. In a little bookstore just across from her she saw a sign:

COMING SOON:
THE NEWEST BOOK BY ALEX ROVER!
NO DETAILS REVEALED UNTIL
PUBLICATION DATE: **14 JULY!**
BUY IT HERE SOON!

'What's the name on the ticket?' the man asked.

'Al—' Alex looked at the sign again and shuddered. 'Alice. Alice Dozer.'

She signed for it quickly, so he didn't notice that it wasn't exactly the same name as on her credit card.

Then she went to the dock to wait for the ship.

'IT'S SIMPLE,' Nim told Fred. 'All we have to do is search the ship and we'll find Selkie.'

The Kids' Klub was in the stern, so they walked past the elevator and the long rows of locked cabin doors to the set of stairs and elevators up front in the bow.

'Up or down?' Nim asked Fred.

Fred couldn't decide, but the animal buttons outside the elevator showed that the Armadillo Deck was the tenth

deck above the water and there were only three more decks above it. The next level up was the Sea Lion Deck.

Aha! Nim thought and raced up the stairs.

They came out into bright sunshine and saw a small pool with a flat rock in the middle and a wall round the edge saying SEA LION DECK.

There were no sea lions inside it.

Grabbing her shell whistle, Nim blew two long, shrill notes that would call Selkie in from the furthest reef at home on the island.

But Selkie didn't come. Nim looked for her in the huge swimming pool with the long, curving waterslide, and in the hot, bubbling pool where people lazed the way Nim liked to float in her own rainforest pool. The only sea lions she could find anywhere were plastic, set out on a giant chessboard with other life-sized animal pieces.

And beyond the ship, whichever way Nim looked, there was nothing but empty sea. Her island was far, far away.

'Even if we find her,' she said to Fred, 'how are we going to get home?'

Fred stared hard.

'You're right!' Nim said. 'The important thing is to find her – we can figure out how to escape once we're all together.'

The next deck up was the Flamingo, where two long-legged, pink birds stood in a shallow pond inside their narrow cage. People at white tables sipped drinks while others whooshed screaming down the waterslide into the

Sea Lion Deck pool. Nim thought about how much Selkie would love the slide. Fred tickled under her chin to say he'd like to try it too.

Upstairs, at the very top of the ship, there was only a half deck, where joggers in shorts ran on a track through an aviary of eagles.

'So now we have to go down,' Nim said. She decided to take the elevator – and even though her stomach still flip-flopped, it wasn't quite so bad now that she knew it was going to happen.

They went down past the Flamingo and Sea Lion Decks, past the Armadillo Deck where the Kids' Klub was, and got out on the Toucan Deck. It had a path outside, where people leaned over the railing to gaze out to sea, and inside it was full of cabins, with a hall down the middle.

In every hall was a cage with the animals the deck was named after. After the toucan were chinchillas and then parrots, but the one that made Nim feel the saddest and sickest of all was the cage with six frightened baby spider monkeys.

But on the Monkey Deck, down the outside path on each side of the ship, was a row of lifeboats hoisted high on strong steel frames, with a cover like a little roof on top of each one. Most were big enough to hold lots of people, but in the middle was a small, inflatable motorboat, like the one that had picked her up this morning, with a canvas cover on top. Exactly like the one that had seal-napped Selkie.

Nim whistled her shell-whistle again, loud and clear

under the boat, and again under the one on the other side of the ship.

There was no answer, not the slightest thump or whuffle.

Nim ran on down to the Butterfly Deck, which was full of rooms with things to buy, and rooms with food and drink – but most of all, full of people. Men and women, old and young, fat and thin, bald and hairy, in bathing suits and white uniforms, in shorts and T-shirts and long silk dresses. People, people, people! Nim thought. It was like being in the middle of sunbaking sea lions, but noisier.

She opened a door to a library full of books and quiet, but she couldn't hide there until she'd found Selkie. Behind another door, amidst a roomful of smiling people, a woman with a long white dress and flowers in her hair was walking up the aisle to a man who looked so happy he was nearly crying.

A wedding! Nim thought. I'm seeing a real wedding!

She felt like crying too, but not because she was happy.

Nim and Fred looked in cafes and restaurants, beauty salons and barbershops, dress shops and pyjama shops, sports shops and toy shops. On the next deck, they watched a cougar snarling as it paced its cramped cage in a room with bright lights and red velvet. They searched in video arcades, bars and theatres. They were back down on the deck where they'd come on board, but there was still no sign of Selkie.

Fred rubbed his spiky back against Nim's neck.

'You're right,' she said. 'We'll find her. We just have to keep going.'

DOWN THE STAIRS Nim ran, past the Piranha Deck where Kylie's cabin was, down to the lowest deck of all.

There weren't any people on this deck; the engine's deep rumble was louder and thumped more strongly through her feet, with a smell that reminded her of the seaplane. And instead of a painting of an animal at the bottom of the stairs, this sign said:

CREW ONLY! NO PASSENGERS ALLOWED!

Nim put on her Troppo Tourist jacket.

A man in grey overalls came out of a doorway. 'What are you doing here?' he demanded.

'I'm . . . I'm taking him back to the Professor,' Nim said, pointing to Fred on her shoulder.

'His door's behind you.'

'Thanks!' said Nim, hoping he wouldn't hear her heart, which was thumping as hard as her feet on the steel floor. She turned to the door that said:

FOUNDATION FOR RESEARCH ON INTELLIGENT,
UNIQUE AND INTERESTING ANIMALS
DANGER: KEEP OUT.

Nim went in.

5

THE ROOM WAS full of cages and sad smells. There were
parrots, songbirds, lizards, spider monkeys, a tank of
tropical fish – and Selkie, lying in a cage beside an old
bathtub full of dirty seawater.

Nim raced across the room, yanked open the cage door
and threw herself onto the sea lion, hugging and kissing
her, rubbing her head and tickling her whiskers. Selkie
whuffled and opened her eyes.

'It's okay, Selkie,' Nim whispered. 'I've come to–' but
before she could finish the sentence, a deep voice snarled,
'Hey! What are you doing here?'

Nim looked up at a tall, pale man with steel-blue eyes.
Nim didn't recognize him, but Jack would have and so
would Alex. The Professor had been on the Troppo Tourist
boat that scared Nim's mother's whale to the bottom of the
sea, and on the one that had dropped off Alex and her tiny
boat in the terrible storm when Jack was lost at sea and Alex
came to rescue Nim.

All Nim knew was that he was the person who'd

seal-napped Selkie. She was as angry as Fire Mountain before it erupted.

But she also knew she'd never get Selkie out of here if she let that fire escape.

'Are you the Professor?' she asked.

He nodded. 'How did you get down here?'

'I want to work with the animals,' said Nim.

The Professor laughed. 'Let me guess: your mum's on the crew, she smuggled you on board and now you're bored!'

Nim nodded as if he'd guessed her secret.

'What's your mum's name?'

'Alex,' said Nim and then she felt even worse. Her mother's name had been Emily.

'And will she think it's a good idea for you to be snooping around down here?'

'She knows I like learning about animals,' Nim said quickly. 'And . . . and I thought you'd like to see this marine iguana.'

Fred stared fiercely.

'That,' said the Professor, 'is the ugliest thing I've ever seen.

Luckily, some people like ugly. Find an empty cage and stick it in.'

Fred tucked himself tighter around Nim's neck.

'HE'S NOT GOING IN A CAGE!' Nim said. 'Animals don't belong in cages!'

The Professor's voice was like ice. 'The Foundation for Research into Intelligent, Unique and Interesting Animals helps animals from all over the world. The most intelligent, unique or interesting will go to millionaires' homes – I mean, be relocated in appropriate environments – at the end of the cruise.'

'But . . . the iguana could learn to be even more intelligent, unique and interesting if he stays with me!'

The Professor shrugged. 'Suit yourself – as long as you remember that all the animals on this ship are the property of the Foundation. But if you want to tame him, I guess I can allow that.'

'We've already put on a show for the Kids' Klub.'

He laughed, a thin sort of laugh. 'So you fancy yourself a mini-Professor, do you? Think you could take over my job of giving animal lectures to the passengers?'

'No, no, of course not! It was just a little show for the kids. But I could help you . . . I've even worked with sea lions before. I bet I could teach that one all sorts of tricks!'

'That sea lion,' the Professor said, 'is a mean, vicious beast. It tried to bite me when I rescued it. It'll be more cooperative after a few days with no food.'

Nim felt as if someone had thrown a coconut hard against her stomach. She took a deep breath. 'Think, think!' she told herself. 'All that matters is helping Selkie!'

'Sea lion,' she announced to the cage, 'your name is . . . Selkie! Selkie, come out!'

'You can't do that!' the Professor bellowed as he jumped out of Selkie's way.

'Selkie,' Nim began.

The Professor grabbed a long whip from the corner of the room.

Nim looked around wildly. There was nowhere to hide. 'Don't you hit her!' she screamed and leaped in front of her friend.

'We'll get out of this somehow,' she whispered to Selkie. 'Just do what I say, even if it seems stupid.'

'Get away from her,' the Professor snarled.

Nim ignored him. 'Selkie: handstand!'

Selkie raised herself on her front flippers and did her best handstand.

What next? Nim thought desperately.

Fred scurried across to Selkie. He rolled himself into a ball.

'Oh, Fred!' said Nim.

Fred rolled himself tighter.

'Selkie,' said Nim. 'Football!'

Selkie sat thinking with her head on one side, the way she did when something was tricky. Nim always shouted at her when she threw Fred instead of the coconut when they played football, and Fred always sulked.

'Football!' Nim said again.

Selkie flicked Fred up with her nose and threw him neatly to Nim. He climbed tight round Nim's neck again.

'Thank you!' said Nim. 'Now, give me a kiss.'

Selkie waddled over and whiskery-kissed Nim on the cheek.

The Professor's eyes opened wide with surprise. He smiled as he put down his whip. 'Okay, girlie, you can help.'

6

JACK SAT ON Selkie's Rock till his shadow stretched dark across the beach – but the little red seaplane never came back and neither did Nim.

'Nim!' Jack called, walking home to the new hut the three of them had built together. Nim and Jack's previous home had been blown away by the terrible storm. 'Nim! Dinner time!'

The only answer was a honk from a sea lion. Jack couldn't tell whether or not it was Selkie.

'Nim!' he called again. 'Nim!'

She wasn't at the hut. She wasn't on Turtle Beach or Shell Beach, or at the rainforest pool or the vegetable garden, or on Sea Lion Point at Keyhole Cove.

She knows Alex has gone! Jack thought. She doesn't want to see me because I somehow drove Alex away. Poor Nim!

He climbed up to the Emergency Cave, because he thought she might hide there if she really didn't want to see him.

There were fresh footprints on the floor, but no Nim. And that's when Jack really started to worry.

48

ALEX SAT so long in the Sunshine Island waiting room that the sea outside the window had turned black. Suddenly the ship floated into the harbour with its lights twinkling like a fairy-tale castle.

Alex didn't care about fairy tales. She just wanted to go to her cabin, lock the door and not come out till she got to the other side of the world.

THERE WERE NO portholes in the Animal Room, but Nim felt the engines stop and the ship bump gently against a wharf.

Now we can escape! Nim thought, rubbing Selkie's head in a get-ready way. Fred was already tucked tight on her shoulder, worn out after his busy day.

'Okay, kid,' said the Professor. 'Time to get that sea lion back into its cage.'

'But . . .'

The Professor pointed his whip at her. 'Let's get things straight. Out of the goodness of my heart, I'm going to let you help me with the animals. But if you don't do exactly what I say, when I say it, I'll have to tell the Captain that your mum brought a stowaway on board. He'll have to tell the police, and you and Alex will have to go to jail.'

Nim nodded.

Nim hugged Selkie hard and it felt like the second worst thing she'd ever done.

Selkie slid slowly into her cage.

'Now, scram. I don't want your mum snooping around here looking for you.'

'She wouldn't do that!' Nim spluttered, though she didn't know if she was defending her mother or Alex.

The Professor laughed, pushed her out of the door and locked it behind him.

There was nothing Nim could do but walk back up the hall and up the stairs as if she knew where she was going.

'Fred,' she whispered, when they were alone. 'What are we going to do?'

Fred made his hungry face, which wasn't any help at all.

Nim got into the elevator, pushed the Armadillo button and went back to the Kids' Klub. No one was there. Nim and Fred curled up in a chair to share the banana in her pocket – but she'd seen two women cleaning the Troppo Tots' room next door, and Nim knew that if they came in here, they'd tell her to get out and go back to her cabin. Even with Fred on her shoulder Nim felt alone, very small and very, very frightened. She needed to find somewhere safe to sleep.

An empty soft drink bottle rolled out from under a chair.

Nim thought of how she and Jack always checked bottles when they drifted in with the tide. 'There might be a message,' Jack always said. So far, there never had been – but they liked imagining that someday there might be.

Paper and pencils were stacked on a desk. Nim peeked out of the door: the women were still washing the Troppo

Tots' floor. She had maybe a minute before they found her.

Dear Jack,

*The Troppo Tourists have seal-napped Selkie. Fred
and I are on the ship too. We will rescue Selkie as soon
as we can but she is locked up tonight.*

I'm very, very sorry I made Alex leave.

Love (as much as Selkie loves fish),

Nim

Nim walked slowly down the stairs to the next deck,
round the walkway that ran right round the ship and then
down to the next and the one after that, because she didn't
know where to go or what else to do. She could see lights
on the wharf and in the houses behind it, as if everyone had
a torch or candles in their windows. It looked like a scene
out of a fairy tale.

Other people were looking out too, leaning on the
railings and chatting. Some of them smiled and said hello,
but Nim kept on walking round to the other side of the
ship. No one was on that side because there was nothing to
look at except the black and empty sea, and nothing to do
unless you were a lonely Nim throwing her message-in-a-
bottle far into the darkness, hoping the waves would float
it to Jack.

She went down the stairs again, to the Monkey Deck,
where the lifeboats were. She stopped under the smaller,
inflatable motorboat.

'Hang on, Fred,' said Nim.

Swinging upside down like a nimble monkey-girl, Nim scrambled up the frame and onto the boat, unclipped one end of the canvas cover and slid inside. Then she pulled out four life jackets to make a mattress and pillow, and curled up.

Fred went straight to sleep, but Nim kept seeing Selkie locked in her cage, and Alex flying away on the plane, and Jack coming happily back from unloading his solar panels to find Alex gone. She didn't know how she was going to save Selkie, or where they were going to end up, or how they were going to live on this ship.

For the first time since she was a baby, Nim cried herself to sleep.

NIM WAS SO tired, and the canvas lifeboat cover kept the light out so well, that she didn't wake up till long after the sun was up and the ship was back out at sea.

She opened her eyes, peeked quickly over the edge of the lifeboat – and ducked down even faster, because a boy was coming out of the cabin in front of her.

Nim settled back down to wait. Fred made a hungry face, so she dug through all her pockets to see what she could find: a pencil and a very soggy notebook, a green stone, six ankle bands for birds visiting the island, a small bamboo cup, a few strands of seaweed . . . and the map Alex had drawn.

She gave Fred the seaweed and, very gently, spread Alex's map out on the seat. It was torn on the fold lines and a bit faded.

'You'll be grounded all the way to New York,' Kylie had said when they pulled Nim out of the sea. New York was where Alex's editor was – the one person in the world who would know where Alex was now.

'Oh, Fred, we're going to rescue Selkie, find Alex – and bring us all together again!' she whispered. 'All we have to do is stay on the ship till the end of the trip – without getting caught.'

Then there was a thump, and a bump, and a boy slithered into Nim's boat.

NIM AND THE boy stared at each other.

Fred and the boy stared at each other.

'Ben!' a girl called. 'What are you doing?'

Ben didn't answer.

'I'm coming up too!'

Nim's boat rocked again and Erin slithered in.

'Be quiet!' Ben hissed. 'She's a stowaway!'

'I thought you were the Professor's kid!'

'I didn't mean to stow away,' Nim said, 'but the Professor kidnapped Selkie.'

'Kidnapped!' Erin and Ben whispered together, crouching closer towards her in the bottom of the lifeboat.

I shouldn't have told them! Nim thought. Now Selkie will stay in that cage forever.

'Who's Selkie?' asked Erin.

'How are you going to rescue her all by yourself?' asked Ben.

SO NIM TOLD them her story. It was hard for Erin and Ben to believe, but they knew it was true.

'We'll help!' said Erin.

'It's not going to be easy,' said Nim. 'We need to make a plan.'

'But first, we all need breakfast,' said Ben. Fred lifted his head and stared. He liked this Ben.

'You exit first, Ben,' said Erin. 'No one's ever surprised to see you popping out of strange places.'

With a quick peek over the edge, Ben swung down and a second later rapped twice on the metal frame to say the coast was clear. Erin followed. After a while there were two more raps and Nim climbed out too. Erin was waiting at the open door of the cabin; Nim could see a man and a woman disappearing down the stairs with two small girls and Ben.

'Come inside, quick!' Erin whispered.

This cabin was bigger and fancier than Kylie's, with two beds and two sets of drawers and lamps, a desk and wardrobe.

'This is Ben's and mine,' Erin said. 'Mum and Dad and the twins are in the cabin next door – but they've gone to breakfast now, so we'll be okay.' She opened the wardrobe. 'I've got some clothes for you.'

'I've already got clothes!' said Nim.

'Your shorts are great,' Erin said, 'but if you're going to hide on the ship, you need to look like the other kids.'

Erin was right, Nim thought. A disguise was more important than wearing her own clothes.

In the bathroom, Erin gave Nim a bag with a

toothbrush, a tiny tube of toothpaste and a comb. 'We got these on the plane. Meet us at the Kids' Klub after you've visited Selkie – we'll bring you breakfast.'

Erin raced out to meet up with her family and Nim had a shower. This time she closed the shower door so Fred couldn't run in and out, and not much water got on the floor. She hung her towel up where Erin had shown her, changed into her new clothes and slipped out of the cabin, her rubber sandals flip-flopping a strange music on her feet.

The Animal Room was still locked. Nim sat outside the door, calling to Selkie through the crack, but she couldn't hear any sea lion whuffles on the other side. Finally, the Professor came to unlock it, yawning and grumbling.

Selkie was sitting up in her cage, looking cross and bored. Nim rushed to her.

'Never hug the animals!' the Professor snarled.

'But it helps them learn tricks,' said Nim.

The Professor grunted. 'So what do you think you could teach them?'

'I'll bet the sea lion could catch fish,' said Nim.

Selkie barked yes.

Nim threw two fish high and twirling and Selkie caught them both.

'That's enough,' snapped the Professor. 'She needs to be hungry enough to learn something more interesting.'

'She could do much better tricks if she was in the water,' said Nim.

The Professor pointed to the bathtub.

'That's not big enough!' But Selkie slid into it, because if she rolled and splashed at least she could get wet.

'She's just too fat!' the Professor sneered.

Selkie glared and slid out of the tub – and Fred scrabbled from Nim's shoulder into the bit of water left behind, checking for seaweed.

Nim threw a fish into the tub. Fred didn't eat fish, so he flicked it over the edge to Selkie. Selkie opened her mouth and the fish disappeared.

'If they had a pool to practise in,' said Nim, 'I could teach them fantastic tricks.'

'Hmph,' said the Professor. Nim wished she knew what that 'hmph' meant, but at least he let her give Selkie the rest of her breakfast fish. She put out seeds for the birds too and fruit for the monkeys and lizards, but most of the animals cowered at the back of their cages, too frightened to eat.

Fred clung tight to Nim's shoulder. He was too afraid of being locked up to even steal food from the caged lizards.

Selkie stuck close to Nim's side, whuffling worriedly. She was afraid of being locked up again too, but she was more worried about what the bad man might do to Nim.

And so when the Professor ordered Selkie to her cage and Nim out of the room, Selkie didn't complain so that Nim wouldn't worry, and Nim didn't cry so that Selkie wouldn't worry.

Fred just waited till the Professor had gone the other way down the hall, with the key in his pocket – then he sneezed, hard.

AFTER THE GREY misery of the Animal Room, the Kids' Klub seemed like a strange kind of dream, with too many lights and too many colours, too much noise and too many kids.

'Come on,' said Erin, 'let's go outside.'

They ran up the stairs to the Sea Lion Deck. 'The perfect spot for planning a sea lion rescue!' Ben exclaimed.

It was hard not to feel a little happier as they lounged in the deck chairs beside the great blue pool, looking out over the deeper blue sea. Erin gave Nim a peanut butter sandwich on fresh white bread. The peanut butter was sticky, but Nim liked it after the first few bites. Ben had a banana in his pocket that was only a little bit squashed and a piece of watermelon in a napkin that was completely smashed.

Fred loved smashed watermelon.

And as they ate and talked, their plan grew – and grew and grew.

ALEX HAD NO plans at all. Not one.

A young woman with *Virginia* on her nametag knocked on the cabin door with a glass of good morning juice. 'I'm your steward for the trip, Miss Dozer – is there anything I can do to help you settle in?'

'Could you have all my meals sent to my cabin, please?'

'Sure!' said Virginia. 'But I hope you're feeling well enough to get out and do things soon. The Professor's lecturing on spider monkeys this afternoon. Poor little things . . . anyway, the Professor says they don't mind being away from their mothers and he's the expert! Maybe you'll feel well enough to go to that.'

'Maybe,' said Alex. Then she remembered she'd been wearing her same blue T-shirt and red trousers for two days and a night. 'Is there anywhere on the ship to buy clothes?'

Virginia smiled. 'Clothes, jewellery, sports gear . . . we've got absolutely everything!' She handed Alex a phone directory from the desk. 'Do you know there's one old lady who lives on the ship full time? She says she never intends to go ashore again, because the ship has everything a city does – so I'm sure you'll find something you want.'

Alex flipped through the directory and phoned the Troppo Ladies' Leisurewear Shoppe to order a few new pairs of shorts and tops.

But when she opened her mouth, she heard herself ask for pyjamas, because deep down, all she really wanted to do was stay in her bed from now until she had to get off the ship. Or maybe she'd be like the old lady and just stay on the ship for the rest of her life.

JACK HAD SEARCHED for Nim all night, from one end of the island to the other and across the other side. When the sun came up, he was on top of Fire Mountain.

Far below him was the top of Frigate Bird Cliffs, then Turtle Beach's pale-gold sand, the grasslands and Shell Beach at the hut, Sea Lion Point and Keyhole Cove, and finally, the grim, black lava-rock, where the Emergency Cave was hidden.

But no matter which way or how far his binoculars searched, there was no sign of Nim.

'She's not on the island,' Jack finally admitted. 'And Selkie would never let her fall into the sea and drown. She must be with Alex.'

The picture of the seaplane leaving was burned into his mind, but when he tried to decide if he could have seen the top of Nim's wild hair in the back, behind Alex's gold head, sometimes he could and sometimes he just couldn't.

Jack was angry, because they'd left without telling him, and he was frightened for Nim because she'd never been in a city, even though she'd be safe with Alex. But most of all he was sad because he was on the island without them and they were somewhere else without him, and they should all be together.

'I'll simply have to go and find them,' said Jack.

The problem was, he had absolutely no idea where they could be.

TWELVE WEEKS AGO, a storm had taken Jack's boat. The same storm that had brought Alex to the island. The boat never came back – and Jack hadn't yet built a new one.

He'd have to take the seaplane, just like Alex and Nim. With a bit of luck, by the time it got here he'd know where he was going.

Jack ran, slid and skidded, all the way down Fire Mountain back to the hut. He turned on the computer and checked his emails just in case there was one from Alex, and when there wasn't, he wrote one to her.

From: jack.rusoe@explorer.net
To: aka@incognito.net
Date: Friday 9 July, 7:03
Subject: WHERE ARE YOU?

Dear Alex,

Why did you go? Where have you gone?

Why did you take Nim without telling me?

Please give her this message:

Dear Nim,

    Stay with Alex; I'm coming.

    Love, Jack

Then, to make sure Nim knew he meant it, he added,

    (as much as Selkie loves the ocean)

Next he wrote:

From: jack.rusoe@explorer.net
To: delia.defoe@papyruspublishing.com
Date: Friday 9 July, 7:05
Subject: Alex Rover

Dear Delia,

    Alex has disappeared. She's taken Nim. Do you know where she's gone?

    Yours truly,

    Jack Rusoe

Finally, he wrote:

From: jack.rusoe@explorer.net
To: seaplane@sunshineisland.com
Date: Friday 9 July, 7:08
Subject: EMERGENCY!

Please return to the island where you brought supplies this morning. I need to leave immediately.

    Urgently,

    Jack Rusoe

The computer dinged before he'd even had time to
stand up.

From: delia.defoe@papyruspublishing.com
To: jack.rusoe@explorer.net
Date: Friday 9 July, 7:09
Subject: Re: Alex Rover

Thank you for your email. I'm presently out of the
office due to the preparations for the launch of Alex
Rover's exciting new book on 14 July. I can assure
you, it will be worth the wait!

As you can appreciate, there is a large backlog of
emails at this time. However I will endeavour to reply
within ten to fifteen working days.

Regards,

Delia Defoe

'Ten to fifteen working days!' Jack shouted. 'I can't wait
that long!'

The computer dinged again.

From: seaplane@sunshineisland.com
To: jack.rusoe@explorer.net
Date: Friday 9 July, 7:10
Subject: I'm on holiday!

I am going on holiday, so Sunshine Island Seaplane will
be closed from Thursday evening 8th July to Monday
30th August. I hope this doesn't cause any
inconvenience.

This is an automated reply. This mailbox will not be checked until Monday 30th August.

Happy travelling!

Sam

Sunshine Island Seaplane

'How am I going to travel?' Jack shouted.

'And,' he added, as he typed 'Troppo Tourists' into the search box, 'I'M NOT HAPPY!'

Jack thought their island was the most beautiful island in the whole world, with birds and animals who were free and happy. He had tried to hide it from the Troppo Tourists, because he knew that if they came, they'd drive away the birds and animals and pick the plants, and then it wouldn't be the most beautiful island in the world any more.

But here's the thing – Jack loved Nim more than he hated the Troppos. And since they'd once brought Alex nearly all the way from Sunshine Island, maybe they could take him back.

'GOODBYE ADVENTURE CHARTERS! HELLO LUXURY CRUISES! BIGGER AND BETTER IN EVERY WAY!
The Troppo Tourists have said farewell to the charter ship that took you on so many adventurous tours. Why plan a trip yourself when we can do it all for you? Remember: if it's worth seeing, the *Troppo Tourist* can take you there!

So come and join us on our glorious new luxury cruise ship! Click here for schedules.'

JACK DIDN'T BOTHER reading any more. He switched off the computer.

'Luxury cruises!' he muttered as he pulled the sleeping mats away from a wall.

The wall was built of strong bamboo poles, firmly laced together. It was the only one without a door or window. Jack grabbed the axe from behind the hut.

'Here's to happy travelling!' he shouted as he chopped a raft-sized square out of the wall. He nailed a blanket across the hole, to keep out the dust and birds, and dropped an empty bag over the computer and science stuff. 'That'll have to do!' declared Jack.

With a thick rope, he hauled his raft across the sand to Shell Beach. He was hot, tired and thirsty when he finished, but he only stopped long enough to split a coconut and drink its milk. It was strange not to have Fred begging for the coconut meat . . .

Fred might be on a plane! Jack thought and he almost smiled as he raced up the hill to Tabletop Garden.

Jack found two strong, slim lengths of bamboo just the right size for a mast and a crossbar, chopped them down and raced back to the beach. He lashed the crossbar to the mast, cut a neat hole out of the centre of his raft and then, with wires and rope and bits of bamboo, fixed the mast in place.

'At least the sail will be easy,' said Jack. He pulled out a bag he'd unloaded from the seaplane just the day before. In it was a sail for the boat he'd planned to build. It was a

perfect, clean white sail, light and strong enough to catch
any wind – but it was too tall and too wide for his little
makeshift raft.

Jack had never had a brand-new sail before.

He took out his fat, red pocketknife, cut a big square
from the sail and rigged it to the mast.

Jack looked out at the wide, empty sea and his small-sailed raft. It didn't look very big or very strong.

He stuffed six coconuts, a change of trousers and shirt and his toothbrush into the sail bag, dropped his compass into one pocket and his notebook and pen into another, and grabbed two fishing lines, two big containers of water and some bananas.

Finally, he opened a metal box. It hadn't been opened for a long, long time, but his wallet and passport were still there, clean and dry. Jack dropped them into his extra-safe pocket – the one with a loop and a string to tie it shut – and walked out of the hut.

'DO YOU KNOW Alex Rover?' Nim asked Erin, when Ben had gone to buy an ice-cream, because some things are easier to say to one person than two.

'Alex Rover the famous writer?'

'She's my friend,' said Nim. 'And my dad's friend. But I was mean to her, and mean to my dad, and now she's gone.'

'Everybody's mean sometimes,' said Erin, though Nim knew Erin could never be as mean as she had been.

'My dad will be worrying that she'll never come back,' said Nim, 'and he might be worried about me, too. Or . . . he might be glad I'm gone.'

'He won't be glad you're gone,' said Erin.

'I wish I could tell him where I am,' said Nim.

'You could email him from the Computer Room.'

'Parents have to log their kids in,' said Ben, handing them each an ice-cream cone.

'Write down the message and the address,' said Erin, 'and I'll send it.'

'Thanks,' said Nim. 'Whew! I never knew ice-cream was so cold!'

From: erin@kidmail.com
To: jack.rusoe@explorer.net
Date: Friday 9 July, 11:05
Subject: Don't worry!

Dear Jack,

My friend Erin is sending this because I can't go to the Computer Room unless you sign me in.

I hope you got my message in a bottle. I'm on the Troppo Tourist ship heading towards New York.

We have a plan but I don't want to write it down in case someone sees the note when Erin is writing it.

I cleaned out the birdcages this morning and four flaming orange doves had our island's bands on their legs. I didn't know people were allowed to catch animals just because they're intelligent, unique or interesting. The Professor says that's the best way to keep them safe. I don't understand but he doesn't like people asking questions.

Also I don't think he really likes animals.

I'm very very sorry I was mean to Alex and I know I was mean to you sometimes when you were talking to Alex. I wish I hadn't been.

Love (as much as Fred loves Selkie),
Nim

She wrote one to Alex too, but in the end she couldn't bear Erin to read it, so she crumpled it up and put it back in her pocket.

'IT'S PIZZA NIGHT in the Kids' Klub,' Ben said, while Erin was emailing, 'so we can all have dinner there.'

'What's pizza like?' asked Nim.

Ben explained. 'But you can't ask anyone but us stuff like that! They'll guess . . .'

'They'll guess I'm a stowaway?'

'They'll probably just think you're weird,' said Ben, 'and that'll make them notice you. Even more than Fred.'

So when Erin came back, they found a spot behind a big white chest labelled LIFE JACKETS, up near the bow where it was too windy for most people to sit, and Nim got lessons on how to look as if she belonged to parents on a cruise ship.

It was sort of like schoolwork with Jack, except that instead of learning about what turtles ate and how plankton grew, she was learning about what kids ate and what they said; what they did and what they had.

'There's so much stuff!' Nim groaned. 'And so much to learn! How am I going to remember it all?'

'Stick with us,' said Erin. 'Just do what we do.'

As Ben looked at his watch, Nim looked up at the sun. 'But first,' she said, 'it's time for Fred and me to visit Selkie.'

SELKIE AND FRED both knew lots of tricks, but they only did them when they wanted to. It was hard for Nim to make them understand that the only way they were going to outsmart the Professor was to do the tricks Nim wanted, when she asked.

And the Professor was watching. He was in a very bad mood because one of the baby spider monkeys had bitten him while he was giving his lecture.

Nim didn't want him to be angry at Selkie too, so first she fed the birds, chirping quietly to them in their own languages.

'If you make bird noises, they'll never learn to talk!' the Professor snapped. 'Teach them "Pretty Polly"! That's what people pay . . . are interested in.'

Without waiting for an answer, he stomped out of the door. Nim was alone with the animals.

She clucked to the doves once more and rushed to open Selkie's cage. Selkie whuffled and sniffed her all over, as if Nim was the one who'd been seal-napped and locked up.

'We'll get home somehow,' Nim told her. 'Because even

if Alex doesn't like me any more, I know she'll help us get back.'

'Anyway,' she added, 'the important thing is to escape. We've got five days to get ready.'

She looked at Selkie's little cage and the cloudy tub of water, and five days seemed forever.

'If I could just get you into a pool,' she said, 'it wouldn't be so bad.'

Very quietly, she turned the door handle. It wasn't locked. She opened it a crack and peered down the hall.

The Professor was coming.

Nim shut the door quickly. She hugged Selkie hard and just for a minute she thought she was going to cry – but that would upset Selkie more than being in a cage.

And it was crying that got us into this mess in the first place! Nim thought, which suddenly seemed so silly she almost laughed – except now the Professor was in the room again, so instead she clapped.

'Fantastic!' she said as if Selkie had just done the most wonderful trick in the world.

Then she added quickly, in case the Professor asked to see it, 'That's enough training for today.'

The Professor grunted. 'Okay, kid, get the rest of those animals fed and cleaned out. If you do a good job, I'll let you do some more training in the morning.'

'Thank you,' Nim said politely, working as slowly and carefully as she could, because every minute she was here was a minute Selkie wasn't locked in her cage alone.

Suddenly she spotted a key hanging behind the door. It looked just like the Professor's, but she'd seen him drop his into his pocket. This one had to be a spare – and if it was a spare, he might not notice if it was missing.

So Nim brushed the rotten fruit and droppings out of the monkeys' cage, put in clean water and not-quite-rotten fruit and murmured quietly to them, trying not to let them feel how sad and angry she was to see them there.

Finally, she put Selkie back in her cage, sitting beside her for a long moment to rub her head with love and cool water.

'Just remember,' the Professor said, with his sneering smile, 'this place is our little secret. The Foundation's work is very important – much too important for most people to understand. I don't ever want to hear you talking about the animals down here.

'So, my little stowaway friend, just keep your mouth shut and everyone will be happy: I'll get a fat stack of money, the animals will get lovely new homes that appreciate how intelligent, unique and interesting they are – and you and your mum can stay out of jail.'

Nim swallowed hard and nodded. He wanted her to be afraid and she was. More afraid than she'd ever been. She was so afraid that the Professor knew he didn't have to worry about her at all. He sat calmly down in his chair in the corner, opened a can of drink and started to read his newspaper.

'I'll come back in the morning,' Nim whispered.

The Professor grunted and turned a page.

Nim backed to the door – and, as she waved goodbye to Selkie, snatched the key off its hook.

10

THE HARDEST THING about fitting in at Pizza Night, Nim
decided, was acting as if the biggest problem in her life was
getting a piece with pepperoni when she wanted anchovies
(because at least anchovies were fish and tasted a bit like
home).

'It's like swimming with a new pod of dolphins,' she told
Ben and Erin, when they took their pizzas out to the deck
to sit alone.

'I wish I could do that!' Ben exclaimed.

'I wish we could go to your island,' Erin said.

'I wish you could too,' said Nim. Saying it made her feel
hot inside, as if she were betraying Jack – but it was true.
She used to wonder what it would be like to have friends
that could talk. Now she'd found out and she liked it. Nim
wanted to be back on her island more than anything else,
but she didn't want to lose Erin and Ben.

She told them what the Professor had said.

'Jail!' repeated Erin.

'But he's the bad guy!' Ben said fiercely.

'He says he's allowed to catch the animals, because of

75

this Foundation. He says that's the law, because catching them educates people and protects other animals all around the world.'

'And he *is* a Professor,' said Erin.

'And I *am* a stowaway,' said Nim.

'But he's still bad,' said Ben.

'We should ask Mum and Dad,' said Erin.

'No!' shouted Nim. 'He said he'd send me to the Captain if I ever told anyone. I shouldn't even have told you – and if you help me, you'll get into trouble too!'

'We don't care,' Ben said.

'All that matters,' Erin agreed, 'is keeping you safe and getting Selkie free. So we just have to stick to our plan.'

'But the best thing we can do right now,' said Ben, 'is try to look like we're having a good time. Let's get some more pizza!'

Fred rubbed his spiny back against Ben's leg. Fred had mozzarella strings tangled from his grinning mouth to his claws. He liked pizza and he liked Ben more and more.

NIM FELT LONELY, climbing back up into her lifeboat with Fred while Erin and Ben stood watch outside their cabin door.

It felt lonely, and when she'd pulled the cover over, it felt dark – black as the deepest sea.

Then she heard a knocking – the three quick knocks and two slow that were their signal – then the rocking of someone climbing the struts.

Ben stuck his head in to hand her a torch.

Nim turned it on and saw why Erin had looked as if she was going to burst with her own secret when she'd said, 'Sleep tight, Nim!'

The boat had been turned into a bedroom. There were two blankets to sleep on, two towels for covers, a pillow for her and one for Fred, a bottle of water and a banana.

But best of all was remembering the look on Erin and Ben's faces when she'd shown them the key to Selkie's prison. They'd touched it as if it were magic – and even though Nim wasn't a magician, just knowing it was in her pocket made her almost as powerful.

IT WAS SO early the sun wasn't up when Erin rapped three 'Wake up!' knocks on the metal strut.

Still half asleep, Nim dropped her pillows and blankets over the side to Erin, just in case a Troppo Tourist used the boat during the day. Then she swung down to the deck, with Fred following. The cool morning air woke them quickly. While Erin tiptoed back into her cabin to hide the bedding, Nim and Fred raced down to the Animal Room. When there was no one around to step on him, Fred liked walking.

With a quick check that no one was watching, Nim unlocked the door and they slipped inside.

'Hurry!' she whispered to Selkie as she undid the cage. She felt sorry for the others, but she couldn't help them yet.

Selkie galumphed down the hall after her and into the elevator, honking with surprise when it went up. Fred grinned a little wider, as if he'd been doing this since he was hatched.

It was dark and deserted as they came out onto the Sea Lion Deck. They raced to the Waterslide Pool and dived into the clear water.

Selkie snorted and rolled, dived and leaped, round and round the pool as fast as she could. Fred sank to the bottom and came up again, sneezing with disgust because he couldn't find any seaweed.

Nim swam with Selkie and dived with Fred; she couldn't swim as fast as a sea lion or hold her breath as long as a marine iguana, but she liked trying. She didn't know exactly how they were going to escape, but she did know they'd all need to be as strong, as fast and as good at everything as they could possibly be.

The sky began to pale. A man hurried past, buttoning his white chef's jacket.

Nim signed to Selkie and Selkie dived as silently as a whisper. Fred was already down at the bottom again; he was sure there must be seaweed somewhere. Nim kept on swimming and tried not to splash.

'You're up early!' the chef called. 'Trying to beat the rush?'

'Yes,' said Nim and he hurried on by.

Nim knew it was too dangerous to stay any longer. They slipped out and back to the hold, with nothing but a quickly drying trail of water to tell where they'd been.

11

JACK WOKE UP with the sun. He'd steered all night, with a few quick naps in between. Now the daylight showed him that he still had a long, long way to go – there was no sign of land in all this wide, blue sea.

A frigate bird circled low to see if he had any fish. 'Nothing today, Galileo!' Jack called. He wished he could tuck a note into the big bird's leg-band, but even Galileo couldn't find Nim in a city.

For just a minute Jack wondered what he'd do if Nim wasn't with Alex – but he pushed that thought away.

As Galileo disappeared into the sky, Jack shouted, 'You're right, I should put those lines out now! Thanks for reminding me!'

He checked his compass, pointed the sail to head four points further east, threw his fishing lines in and had a drink of water and some coconut for breakfast.

'I'll be with you soon, Nim!' he called.

Then he added more quietly, 'And you too, Alex. I hope.'

ALEX WOKE WITH a start. She was sure someone had

knocked on her cabin door: three quick raps. Then there was a thump of someone jumping onto the deck and whispering.

It was just the children from the cabin next door. She'd heard them during the day; it sounded as if there were two very little girls, a boy and another girl about Nim's age, and maybe even another girl. She could never hear what they said, just the buzz of their voices and thumps from their cabin when they jumped to the floor or dumped things out of cupboards.

Alex wondered what they were like. She wondered if they'd know how to be friends with Nim. Maybe I'd have been better at it if I'd met other kids before I went to the island, she thought.

'Because if you'd been better at it,' she told herself, 'you wouldn't be on this ship right now!'

'And don't you dare cry again!' she added and made herself go back to sleep.

NIM HAD GOT Selkie back just in time. It was now bright, busy daylight and people were swarming everywhere, settling into deck chairs and crowding the rails. One of them would have probably noticed a sea lion galumphing through the ship.

It was busy out on the water too: there were more ships ahead, behind and coming towards them. They were going down a wide river with bright green hills close on either side, and Nim felt tight and closed-in when she could suddenly see only a narrow strip of water instead of the wide blue sea she was used to.

The river became skinnier and the banks grew steeper, until it was such a narrow canal that their ship was nearly touching both concrete sides. Very gently, they were tugged up to a pair of locked giant doors. Another pair of doors shut behind them – and just as Nim was wondering where the ship could go next, it started going up as if it were in an elevator.

Nim tried to look as if she were used to being on ships that went up and down elevators, until she saw that nearly everyone on board had come out to watch and take pictures.

'Amazing!'

'How does it work?'

'The water comes in through culverts from a lake.'

'I've wanted to see this all my life!'

But everything's strange to me! thought Nim. How am I supposed to know which ones are strange to everyone else?

She saw Erin and Ben, with their parents and little sisters, watching from outside their cabin while their mother videoed the giant elevator doors.

Now the dock on the other side of the railing was the same height as the deck. If she jumped over the railing right now, she could probably escape the ship.

'But we can't leave without Selkie,' she whispered to Fred. Fred rubbed his head under her chin.

The ship went up higher and higher till they were way too far above the dock to jump.

Anyway, thought Nim, if we'd got off here, how would I ever find Alex?

And how would I ever find home?

Maybe we'll have to stay on the ship forever and never go ashore again.

THAT AFTERNOON IN the Kids' Klub, Kelvin taught them to play Spiderweb. The person who was Spider stood in the middle with their hands above their head, while all the other kids squashed up in a circle around them. When Kelvin shouted 'Web!' they had to reach behind, grab the first two hands they met and keep on holding them while they all wiggled around, forward and back, to get back into a circle – while the Spider tried to get through to the other side.

'But no hitting or kicking!' Kristie warned. 'Spiders don't hurt their own net!'

Nim was good at being Spider, because she could squirm under arms or slither through legs faster than anyone. But what she liked best was holding tight to Erin or Ben or kids she didn't know and just being part of the web.

From: erin@kidmail.com
To: jack.rusoe@explorer.net
Date: Saturday 10 July, 17:45
Subject: More information

Dear Jack,

I thought you might have answered by now but I guess you are very busy since I'm not there to help you with the science stuff.

Today the Professor took pictures of me holding the birds and cage animals. He says the Foundation likes to see pictures like this to show how intelligent, unique and interesting the animals are, to prove why they should be protected. He dressed one of the spider monkeys up like a baby and I thought it looked silly and it couldn't have swung around even if it wasn't in a cage, but I played a swinging game with it afterwards to cheer it up.

Selkie is a lot happier today because she had a swim in the pool and Fred was happy because he tasted pizza last night and today Ben brought him a whole pocketful of salad for lunch. I've had lots of different food too. Ben and Erin said I shouldn't ask for a seaweed sandwich because people would think that was strange and they might guess I'm a stowaway. It's quite funny because when you want food here you don't have to make it or catch it yourself.

I saw a frigate bird today. I wished it was Galileo with a message from you.

Love (as much as Galileo loves stealing fish),
Nim

'I'VE GOT AN idea,' Nim said, the morning after the ship went through the elevator canal, because the Professor was whistling a cheerful whistle and she needed him to be in a good mood so she could start putting their plan into action. 'You know how you give a lecture about animals every day? When you do the sea lion lecture on Wednesday, it could be like a show – like a circus! And I could help.'

'There's not enough time. I know all there is to know about training animals – it takes months for them to learn to do tricks on command.'

'But this sea lion is amazingly smart – and so is the iguana. I bet I could get them ready for you, especially if I could train them in a pool.'

'That beast will go to the Sea Lion Pool,' snarled the Professor, 'when I'm sure she won't bite anyone else.'

I wish she'd bitten you harder! Nim thought. 'She was probably just scared,' she said. 'I'm positive she won't do it again.'

'She'd better not,' said the Professor, glancing at his whip.

'Everyone could see how intelligent, unique and interesting they both are.'

'Well, maybe we can do a show on Wednesday morning. Then if she behaves, she can stay in the Sea Lion Pool till she's sold . . . till she's relocated.'

Relocated? thought Nim, feeling as if she'd just swallowed a bucket of cold water. How would I ever get her back then?

But we won't let that happen! she reminded herself fiercely. We've still got three days to get our show ready – and then we'll escape.

'You can have a couple of hours in the afternoons to practise. And . . .' the Professor paused and stared at her as if he knew exactly what she was thinking, 'it had better be good.'

'BUT HOW'S IT going to be good if we can't use the big pool?' Nim demanded when she and Erin and Ben were in the Kids' Klub carving watermelons into interesting sculptures. Kristie had demonstrated how to carve a Viking's head and a sailboat, and now each kid had a watermelon and a blunt knife, and could carve whatever they liked.

Nim used her own sharp pocketknife to carve Selkie. Erin carved a cat and Ben made a Viking's head that was nearly as good as Kristie's.

Fred ate the whole middle out of a watermelon and made an empty rowboat. Everyone clapped and he scrambled back onto Nim's shoulder, looking smug.

'Do you think that could be a trick?' Nim asked.

'I don't think so,' said Erin. 'But I *have* figured out how you can use the Waterslide Pool for your show.'

JACK HAD BEEN on his raft for three days. He still had two coconuts and half a container of water, but he was a bit sore, very stiff and very, very tired. It was not a big raft and it was not comfortable at all.

There was a line on the horizon that could have been cloud or . . . Sunshine Island? Jack hoped so.

The closer he sailed the clearer and less cloudlike the line became. By noon he was sure. It was definitely land. Jack tightened the sail and whistled for wind.

A speck of light caught his eye. A bottle was bobbing on the waves – with something inside it.

If Nim had been with him, they would have chased and grabbed it.

But they'd never ever found a message – and if Nim had been with him, he wouldn't be going to Sunshine Island on a raft made out of the wall of their hut. Jack let the bottle float by and sailed on as fast as he could.

ALEX HAD SPENT three whole days alone in her cabin. She hadn't spoken to anyone except Virginia the steward, when she brought her juice every morning, and came back a little later to clean. 'What a shame you're not feeling better!' Virginia said. 'You'd have so much fun if you could get out there and meet people.' But Alex had left behind the only people she wanted to know.

She even kept her curtains closed, because all she could see were people walking by, and the lifeboat stands, which weren't very interesting.

And, even though there were pens and writing paper in her cabin's desk, she hadn't written a word. For the first time in her life, there was no story in her head.

Worst of all, she didn't care.

From: erin@kidmail.com
To: jack.rusoe@explorer.net
Date: Sunday 11 July, 17:30
Subject: Important!

Dear Jack,

Selkie and Fred and I are going to put on a show, so we practised for two hours this afternoon. It's horrible being with Selkie when the Professor's watching because I have to pretend I don't know her, and pretend I'm training her to do tricks, even though it's just the games we play at home. But Selkie thinks it's better than being in the cage so she doesn't mind pretending. Fred hates the Professor so much he just glares at him all the time but the Professor never notices.

It's very interesting being on the ship but I still like our island better. I hope you will stop being mad at me soon.

Love (as much as Jack loves the island),
Nim

'No message yet,' Erin said to Nim when she came back from sending Nim's email to Jack. She tried to sound as if it wasn't important, as if she didn't know that Nim was worrying whether Jack was too angry to answer or if there was another reason that was even worse.

'Maybe he keeps forgetting to charge the battery,' Nim said.

'Probably,' said Erin.

'Or a virus!' said Ben.

'Maybe,' said Nim.

'We've got an hour before dinner,' said Ben. 'Let's play Spy.'

'Dolphin Deck?' asked Erin.

'Butterfly,' said Nim and started up the stairs. She always went first when they played Spy, because it was harder for someone with an iguana on their shoulder to blend into a crowd.

She chose the Butterfly Deck, because the butterflies were the only animals on the ship that didn't make her feel sad. They had plenty of space to fly around and she loved it when they landed on her hair and arms. Nim wandered slowly through the butterfly cage, with Fred sitting so still that her head and Fred's spine were soon covered with brightly coloured butterflies. They both smiled so much that even the happy, kissy people, who came in from the wedding room to have their pictures taken, didn't notice that she didn't belong in their party.

13

FROM ONE END of Sunshine Island to the other, people stared as Jack sailed his raft past the roaring jet skis, through the swimmers and snorkellers in the calm water and right up onto the beach between the sunbathers and sandcastles.

He pulled down the sail and folded it into its bag, in case he needed it again. Curious people gathered around.

'Where's the airport?' Jack asked.

Someone pointed down the road.

Someone else took his picture.

'It's a long walk,' one man said. 'I'll drive you.'

Jack followed him to a golf buggy parked at the top of the beach and the crowd drifted back to their sunbathing and sandcastles.

But when they reached the airport: 'You're in luck!' said the man at the airport ticket counter. 'You can get on a flight tomorrow morning.'

'I need to go today!' said Jack.

'Tuesdays and Thursdays – that's it.'

Thursday! thought Jack. That's the day Alex and Nim left. If they missed the flight, they'll still be here.

The man with the golf buggy drove him all around the town till late at night, but they never found a sign of Alex or Nim.

'YOU,' SAID ALEX to herself as she sat cross-legged on her bunk to eat her dinner, 'are a lazy lay-a-bed slobby slug. You've gone through the Panama Canal without even seeing it. What if you need a Hero to stow away on a ship on a great ocean adventure – how are you going to write about it?

'Same way I always do,' she answered. 'Reading, research and imagination.'

'Except the last book,' said Alex. 'You lived that one. That's why it's your best story – and the best part of your life.'

But she hadn't been brave enough to open it yet.

KIDS' KLUB FINISHED at five o'clock, but a big bunch of kids were out on the Sea Lion deck when Erin, Nim and Ben wandered up there after dinner. Nim had just finished eating her smuggled food when a small, pigtailed girl tapped Ben on the shoulder. 'Spider!' she shouted.

Quick as a wink, everyone else grabbed the nearest hands to make the web; Ben wriggled and squirmed to get through and the others held tight until the small, pigtailed girl began to giggle and they all collapsed together in a wiggling, giggling heap, happy as a pile of sea lion pups in the sun.

LATER THAT NIGHT, with her windows open to catch the breeze, Alex heard the next-door parents chatting on the deck after their children had gone to bed. She imagined them leaning over the rail to watch the moonlight dancing on the waves.

'The kids seem to be having a good time,' the father was saying. 'They've made lots of new friends.'

'And they're certainly enjoying the food! They keep heaping their plates with more than they could possibly eat, but when I look again, it's gone.'

'This fresh sea air's certainly giving them an appetite,' the father agreed.

THE NEXT MORNING, Nim, Selkie and Fred sneaked up even earlier to swim in the Waterslide Pool. With the three of them all together, they felt almost free.

At the first sounds of the crew bustling around, they scurried back to Selkie's prison. A few moments later, the ship dropped anchor in a white sand harbour.

Nim locked Selkie in and ran upstairs to say good morning to the dolphins in the fountain. When she went back to the Animal Room, the Professor was waiting for her to start feeding and cleaning.

'No time for that!' he snapped when Nim hugged Selkie. 'Feed them and get out. I don't want you around today.'

'But you said I could practise this afternoon!'

'I've changed my mind. Now snap to it and then scram!'

His eyes were narrow, his face was hard – and he kept glancing at his whip. Nim fed the animals and got out.

'EVERYONE'S GOING ASHORE,' Erin told Nim. 'I wish you could come, but they check the tickets extra carefully when people get back on. It wouldn't be safe.'

'They'll probably use your inflatable,' Ben added. 'Did you get all your things?'

Nim nodded. Everything was tucked safely into Erin's wardrobe.

'The Kids' Klub is shut too,' Erin said sadly, 'so you'd better stay in our cabin.'

Nim had to wander up and down the deck while Erin and Ben's mother hurried in and out of the cabins to organize their day. She felt as empty as a pricked balloon when Ben and Erin finally disappeared down the stairs with their family.

A second later, Erin came running back down the hall.

'I said I forgot my hat,' she puffed, unlocking the cabin door. 'There are some books on my bed, if you want to read, and television, and paper and felt-tip pens for making the posters. I *wish* you could come!'

Erin grabbed her hat, shouted, 'Bye!' and ran out. Nim started looking through the books. One was *Mountain Madness*, by Alex Rover. Nim remembered when she first read it, when she was alone on the island and Alex had emailed to ask Jack about coconuts. Alex had tried to tell Nim she wasn't really the Hero of her story, but Nim hadn't believed her. She wondered if she would still like the book now she knew Alex was just a small, scared woman who'd sailed across the world to help Nim, before she even knew her.

She lay on Erin's bed and started reading.

There was a knock and Ben bounced in. 'We forgot to tell you – breakfast is in the desk!'

He raced out again and Nim found a brown-bread sandwich and an apple in the drawer.

Fred didn't like brown bread and he didn't like apples, but he was hungry enough to share. 'We'll find you something,' Nim said, though she wasn't sure what.

They had a shower; Nim changed into the clothes Erin had left for her and sat down at the desk with the papers and coloured pens. She drew twenty-two SEA LION CIRCUS posters – two for each passenger deck – exactly how she'd planned them with Erin and Ben. When she'd finished, she tucked them neatly into the desk drawer, flopped back onto Erin's bed and went on reading.

Rap! Tap!

Someone was knocking at the door.

Nim stayed very still and didn't answer. Fred crept behind a lamp and went to sleep.

The door opened and a steward in a white uniform and blue apron came in with a vacuum cleaner and a mop and bucket. She saw Nim and dropped her bucket.

'Yipes!' Virginia squeaked. 'Did your parents leave you here alone?'

Nim nodded, because she couldn't tell the truth.

'Are you sick?'

Nim nodded again.

Virginia shook her head sympathetically. 'Sorry – I still have to clean,' she said, 'but I'll be as quiet as I can.'

She straightened Ben's bed and made Nim sit on it while she changed Erin's. 'Leaving a sick child alone!' Nim heard her muttering. 'Appalling!'

Nim thought about Erin and Ben's parents, and her face grew as hot and red as the lava in Fire Mountain. 'I'm feeling a lot better now!'

Virginia finished cleaning, felt Nim's forehead and made her go back to bed.

Nim picked up *Mountain Madness* again. She read lying down, she read sitting up and she read lying on the floor with her feet on the bed. Then she practised doing handstands and Fred practised climbing from her shoulder to her feet instead of the usual way around. They even made up a trick with Fred staying stiff as a log and Nim twirling him around on her feet.

But you can't stay upside down spinning an iguana forever, so after that Nim stared out through the lifeboat stands at a bit of blue sea. A great black frigate bird soared past. Looking through her spyglass she was almost sure it was Galileo. 'I wish I could go out on deck to check,' she muttered, even though she didn't have a fish to call him with.

One more chapter of *Mountain Madness*; the Hero had just caught a trout in a mountain stream and cooked it over a fire.

'I should have saved the apple for lunch,' Nim told Fred. Fred answered with his best unblinking stare. He was sure she could find them some food if she tried hard enough.

'We can't go out,' she told him, 'because everyone else has gone ashore, and the crew will notice me and ask where my parents are.'

There was another knock at the door. Nim shoved a pillow over Fred and Virginia tiptoed in carrying a tray.

'I wasn't sure what you liked,' she said, 'so I brought sandwiches and salad, fruit, cake . . .'

The pillow wiggled. Nim put her elbow on it. 'Thank you. That's very nice of you.'

She was glad she could say something that wasn't a lie.

'I'm so pleased you're starting to feel better. The poor lady next door hasn't left her cabin for the whole trip!'

This cabin was a bright room with cheerful paintings on the walls, but Nim thought she'd have gone crazy if she'd spent the whole trip in it.

'You look a bit bored,' Virginia said as she left. 'Do you want the TV on?' She handed Nim the remote control.

'Thanks,' said Nim.

But even though Nim had seen televisions in the lounges when they played Spy, and she'd played video games in the Kids' Klub, she'd never sat and watched a programme with a story – and she'd never had the remote. Neither had Fred. Fred didn't care about the programmes, but he liked stepping on the buttons so that the channel changed just as Nim figured out what was happening.

'Stop it, Fred!' Nim shouted.

Fred went to sulk under the bed and Nim turned the TV off. She didn't want to shout again and wake up that poor sick lady next door.

'Come on . . . you can have all the lettuce,' she coaxed and when Fred had eaten the lettuce out of the sandwich and sneezed a kiwi fruit all over the bed, he felt quite cheerful again.

Nim finished *Mountain Madness* and stared out of the window some more.

When she heard the rumble of the launches and the thump of passengers' feet on the gangplank, she grabbed Fred and raced outside to gulp deep breaths of fresh air.

And as soon as the ship was on its way out to sea again, Nim pulled on her Troppo Tourist jacket and ran down the stairs to the Animal Room. She waited outside the door until the Professor let her in.

Selkie whuffled sadly, because it had been an even longer day for her. And scarier.

The last of the empty cages was full now – with long, fat snakes.

From: erin@kidmail.com
To: jack.rusoe@explorer.net
Date: Monday 12 July, 19:30
Subject: Very important!

Dear Jack,

Maybe there's something wrong with the computer and that's why you're not answering, but I think you'd want to know what we're doing so I'll go on emailing and maybe you can read it later.

Today I had to stay inside the cabin all day and it was very boring but now I understand even better how Selkie must be feeling, and all the other animals with her. So maybe it was good in some ways.

Erin bought me a bead bracelet when she went ashore. It's very pretty and she bought one for herself just the same so whenever we wear them we will think about each other. Ben brought Fred and me a coconut, which was good because we haven't had coconut for way too long.

Love (as much as Fred loves coconut),
Nim

Sea Lion Circus!

Wednesday 9am
Waterslide Pool

15

JACK SPENT THE night on the floor of his new friend's living room.

'Who are you?' the man joked, when he saw Jack staring at the television as if he couldn't remember what it was. 'Robinson Crusoe?'

'No – Jack Rusoe.'

His friend laughed, but Jack couldn't. He'd just checked his emails – and not one message had come into the Inbox. Only the Trash folder had blinked as the Spam trickled in to be deleted.

The next morning he sorted out how to get money at the bank and took the little plane to the airport on Isla Grande.

The only thing he could do now was to go and see Delia Defoe. She wasn't just Alex's editor – she was probably the only person in the world who knew where Alex was.

There was one seat left on the plane leaving the next day for New York City.

'THERE'S A SEA LION circus tomorrow,' Virginia told Alex when she brought in her breakfast. 'There are posters all over the ship – doesn't that sound fun?'

If Alex hadn't known Selkie, she might have thought it sounded fun. But she did know Selkie and suddenly she missed her so much that she knew she could never see another sea lion again without crying. It was the best reason so far for staying in her cabin another day.

ERIN WOKE NIM and Fred up earlier than usual, but they spent so long in the pool that the sun had come up before they knew it. When Nim came up for air after practising swimming underwater, a white-uniformed crewman was standing at the edge, watching.

'There's a sea lion in there!' he exclaimed.

'It's the Sea Lion Deck,' said Nim.

'But this is a swimming pool. For people.'

'We need it to practise for the sea lion circus,' said Nim. 'We won't need it after tomorrow.'

'The cruise ends tomorrow!'

'That's why we won't need it,' said Nim.

The crewman stared a little longer, then shrugged and walked away.

Nim and her friends scrambled out of the pool and back to the Animal Room as fast as they could.

'I SUPPOSE YOU think you're clever!' the Professor snarled when he let Nim in to feed the animals. 'All those posters advertising a sea lion circus at the Waterslide Pool – now you think I'll have to let that beast in there!'

102

'I must have got mixed up!' said Nim, even though the posters were exactly how she wanted them. 'Isn't that what you meant?'

'I said you could have her perform a few tricks at my lecture. You know perfectly well it was supposed to be in the theatre, like all my lectures. I'm a professor – that's what people expect.'

'I just thought . . .'

'Think about what's going to happen to you and your mum if you try to be smart. Besides, no one's going to look at humdrum animal tricks once we get into the harbour. You'd better do something spectacular or you won't have an audience.'

'I've got a plan,' said Nim. 'It'll be spectacular.'

'THE POSTERS WORKED!' Nim said as Erin handed her a breakfast scrambled-egg sandwich and Ben tossed grapes for Fred to catch. 'We can do the show the way we planned.'

'So today . . .'

'We can do whatever we like.'

It was hard to choose, because even though in some ways today was exactly like every other day on the ship, it was the last day they were going to spend together and that made it special – sad and a little bit scary.

Fred chose to spend the day at the Splash Pool, where he could sit on the water jets and be blasted into the air and then paddle across the pool, just the way he liked to do where the spray came in at a blowhole at the Black Rocks.

Ben, Erin and Nim went on a treasure hunt with the other kids from the Kids' Klub. The clues took them all over the ship, but when Nim got to the Toucan Deck she found the toucan sitting on the floor of its cage. Its eyes were glazed, and it still hadn't touched the food it had been given that morning

Nim squatted down to see it. It's so unhappy it might die! she thought. Suddenly she knew that escaping with Selkie was not enough. Every animal on the ship had to be rescued.

'Just hang in there a little bit longer! We're going to help you somehow,' Nim told the unhappy bird, chirping and clucking until it lifted its head to see her. When it finally began to peck its mushed mango, Nim stood up – and noticed the treasure chest hidden behind the display. It was full of enough bags of sweets for everyone in the Kids' Klub.

Fred thought he liked sweets, but he felt sick afterwards and had to lie on his back while Nim rubbed his tummy.

Then Nim and Erin painted all the papier mâché fish they'd been making and Ben finished his sculpture.

'Excellent!' said Kristie.

'It *is* pretty good,' Erin admitted.

'It's amazing,' said Nim.

But Fred hated it, because it looked exactly like him. He walked all around it, glaring, and then climbed up to Nim's shoulder to glare some more.

'It's so I'll remember you when you're not around,' Ben explained.

Fred blinked, but Nim thought she might cry.

LATER IN THE afternoon, down in the prison, Selkie and Nim practised handstands and Fred practised spinning on Selkie's flippers. It wasn't the most important trick, but it was the start of something bigger.

'Sleep tight,' Nim whispered to Selkie when it was time to leave. 'Everything happens tomorrow.'

From: erin@kidmail.com
To: jack.rusoe@explorer.net
Date: Tuesday 13 July, 17:36
Subject: You must read this!

Dear Jack,

I haven't had an email from Alex yet either so if she is still angry at me too this might be the last email I can write to you. I don't know what I'm going to do but I can't worry about it because first we have to get off the ship. Sometimes I wish you could sail up to the ship and rescue us, but you don't have a boat any more so I know you couldn't do that even if you weren't angry at me.

The Professor made me cut the bands off the island doves' legs today. But if our plans go right it won't matter. Also I've made notes in my notebook about the birds' markings so we can identify them again. I've made notes about all the animals on the ship because I thought you would want me to do that.

A frigate bird has been following the ship for the last three days. It's been flying too high for me to be sure but I think it really is Galileo.

I hope I'll see you and our island again soon.

Love (as much as Selkie loves diving),

Nim

There was a special Kids' Klub dinner for the last night of the cruise so, for the first time, Nim ate in the dining room with her friends. She borrowed a skirt and top from Erin and brushed her wild hair till it was nearly neat. Fred was sleepy, so he crawled under Ben's bed to rest.

'Are you sure you don't want to come?' Nim asked, but Fred just blinked and went back to sleep.

Her shoulders felt light and empty without him, but it made blending in easier.

Which was important because, after the dinner with the other Klub Kids, Nim was going to spend the night in Ben and Erin's cabin.

'Your dad doesn't mind you sleeping over?' their mum asked.

'No,' said Nim, because it didn't seem as if Jack minded about her at all, and if he did, he'd probably rather she slept in a cabin than on the floor of a lifeboat.

Erin loaned her some pyjamas and they squashed into the bed together. Fred stayed under Ben's bed. Nim didn't know if it was to say goodbye to Ben or because he was just too sound asleep to move.

They talked and talked in the darkness. None of them wanted to think about tomorrow, but there was still plenty to talk about till Mr and Mrs Caritas came in to say goodnight.

'DON'T TALK TOO late,' Mr Caritas said. 'It's a big day tomorrow. Do you live in New York, Nim?'

'No,' said Nim. 'It's my first visit.'

'You'll love it! But for us the holiday's over: we'll be going straight to the airport to fly home.'

Their mum bent to kiss Erin on the forehead and then she kissed Nim too. It felt just like when Alex used to kiss her goodnight.

Alex! Nim thought into the night, but even in her head she couldn't quite sort out all the things she wanted to say, so she sent the wish out in a big jumble of love, sorriness and hope.

Ben's voice trickled off into soft snores, but Erin and Nim whispered still.

The door opened quietly. 'You really have to go to sleep now,' said Erin's mum, 'or Nim will have to go back to her dad.'

'That's what you're trying to do!' Erin whispered when the door closed again and they started to giggle. They giggled so hard they had to put the pillows over their heads and then Erin went to sleep.

ALEX HEARD NIM calling – and then she heard her giggle. She was wide awake and at the door before she realized she must have been dreaming again.

But it seemed so real! she thought.

Nim! she thought into the night, but even in her head she couldn't quite sort out all the things she wanted to say, so she sent the wish out in a big jumble of love, sorriness and hope.

NIM STOPPED WORRYING and wondering, and fell fast asleep.

16

NIM HUGGED ERIN and Ben goodbye. They'd see each other later, but they wouldn't be able to talk. She gave Ben her green stone and Erin the bamboo cup that had been in her pocket when she jumped off the cliff. Finally, she gave Ben the bird bands, the Troppo Tourist jacket and, most important of all, the key.

Then she dressed in her own clothes – her bright blue shirt and baggy red trousers with drawstring ties and useful pockets – and went down to the Animal Room. She gave the cage animals love and breakfast, trying to let them feel her hope: 'You'll be free soon!'

By nine o'clock there were more butterflies in her stomach than on the Butterfly Deck. It was time for the circus.

The Professor picked up his whip.

'You don't need the whip,' Nim said bravely. 'Grown-ups won't like it and it will scare the kids.'

The Professor flicked a warning crack. 'Then you'd better keep those animals under control – because I'll be keeping it close at hand, just in case.'

Nim shut her mouth so hard her teeth hurt. It was the only way she could stop herself from shouting every bad name she'd ever heard. She opened the door.

'Selkie, walk!' she ordered. 'Fred, follow!'

'Sorry,' she whispered as they started down the hall. 'After today, I'll *never* talk to you like that again!'

Selkie looked at her with her head on one side and Nim knew she understood, but Fred scuttled along behind looking as cross as an iguana can possibly look.

It was a tight squash in the elevator because none of them wanted to be next to the Professor and his whip. He got out at the Sea Lion Deck, but Nim, Selkie and Fred went up to the Flamingo Deck above, where the cafe chairs were set up around the top of the waterslide, like a theatre balcony for the show at the pool below.

There was a person in every chair and when Nim looked down, she saw people sitting all around the Waterslide Pool and standing behind all the way out to the railings. There were more people than Nim had thought could fit on the ship. For a minute she wanted to turn and run. Fred forgot his sulks and raced up her leg to her shoulder.

Then the three friends walked through the cafe to the top of the waterslide.

Fred rubbed his spiny head under her chin. Nim put her hand on Selkie's shoulder. They were ready. They looked down to see the Professor on a stage beside the pool.

'Ladies and gentlemen!' he shouted. 'Instead of my

usual lecture this morning, I'll be demonstrating how well I've trained a seal and a lizard – by allowing a mere child to do the show!'

Dozens of kids waved and screamed, 'Me! Pick me!'

The Professor ignored them and sat down in a chair near the box, his whip across his knees. 'This had better be good!' he snarled.

FRED WHIZZED DOWN the waterslide into the pool. Nim followed – and then Selkie whooshed down the curves and *whumphed* in with a tidal-wave splash. The audience squealed, clapped and cheered. The people in the front three rows were soaked.

Nim climbed out of the pool to the front stage. She took a deep breath and wondered if her voice would come out at all.

Then she saw Erin and Ben in the very front row – and beside and behind them, all the kids from the Kids' Klub. Suddenly she knew she could do it.

'Ladies and gentlemen!' she shouted. 'Allow me to present my sea lion friend, Selkie!'

Selkie pulled
herself up on the
side of the pool and
bowed her head to the left,
to the right and straight ahead.
Everyone in the audience felt as if
she'd bowed to them.

'And,' Nim continued, 'the handsomest,
funniest, smartest marine iguana in the whole
world: Fred!'

Fred had to scramble up the steps and onto Nim's
shoulder before he could nod at the audience, but when

he did, Erin and Ben cheered so loudly that everyone else had to join in.

'Statue!' Nim shouted and Selkie sat up as tall and still as the plastic sea lions on the giant chessboard.

Nim threw four fish and Selkie expertly caught every one. Fred caught lettuce and chunks of fruit.

'Yay, Fred!' the kids all cheered.

Selkie kissed Erin and Fred sneezed on Ben.

'Yuck, Fred!' the kids all called, laughing as they clapped.

Selkie, Nim and Fred dived into the pool and played coconut football with a ball instead of a coconut.

'Hooray!' shouted the audience.

The ship was going slowly down a strait between mainland and islands. High in the distance was a dark speck that just might be a frigate bird.

'Throw the ball here!' the kids all shouted, until the Professor got out of his seat to glare at them.

Nim hopped out of the pool and threw a rubber ring back in. Fred nosed it up from the bottom and Selkie tossed it back.

'Throw something into the pool!' Nim called. 'And they'll play catch!' A boy threw in his watch. 'It's waterproof!' he shouted and the crowd cheered as Selkie tossed it back.

Nim looked at Erin. Erin nodded and threw in a banana.

Fred grabbed it, Selkie threw it – and Fred gulped it.

'Hooray for Fred!' Kelvin cheered. He still didn't want to touch Fred, but he was glad he'd rescued him.

Out of the corner of her eye, Nim saw Ben slip away from the crowd and down the stairs, pulling on the Troppo Tourist jacket as he ran.

She also saw that the black speck in the sky had grown into a frigate bird outline.

There was only one fish left in the bucket.

But then Erin pulled out the basket of papier mâché fish she and Nim had made. She threw the first one to Nim, twirling it high in the air. Nim caught it and threw it the same way to Selkie, who tossed it to Fred, who tossed it back to Nim as Erin threw the next one to Selkie.

The Professor stood up to take a picture, his whip tucked under his arm.

Nim threw the fish to him.

The crowd gasped as an enormous black bird, wings as wide across as the Professor was tall, swooped in to snatch the papier mâché fish. The Professor gasped and ducked as the bird's left wing brushed his face and its head went through the loop of the dangling whip.

'Introducing Galileo!' Nim shouted, throwing him the last real fish for a reward.

Galileo dropped the papier mâché fish onto the Professor's head, caught the real one and soared upwards with the whip bouncing on his bright red chest – till it slipped away and sank into the cold waters of New York Harbour.

The Professor bellowed with rage. He was so angry he forgot to even pretend that he was in charge of the show.

'If you planned this . . .' he screamed at Nim.

Selkie leaped up and smashed down so hard in front of him that the front rows got soaked all over again. The Professor was drenched, standing in a puddle of water.

'I'm warning you!' he shrieked.

'Play nicely, Selkie!' said Nim and threw her the ball again.

Selkie leaped up as she hit the ball back, straight and hard at the Professor. He threw his arms up to catch it, skidded in the puddle of water and fell down hard on his bottom.

Fred scurried to Selkie's head and sneezed in the Professor's face.

The audience laughed and cheered as if it were a clown act.

'Naughty Selkie!' Nim said lovingly. 'Naughty Fred!'

'Yuck, Fred!' the kids shouted gleefully.

Selkie whuffled and put her flippers up to her face as if she were crying.

The audience cheered louder than ever.

The Professor's eyes went narrow and his face was purple red. 'That's the end of the show!' he shouted.

Now the ship was going under a bridge. The land was close enough that they could see the cubes and rectangles of buildings, but there was still a bit further to go.

'Encore!' shouted Erin and the whole audience took it up, 'Encore, encore! More, more, more!'

Nim blew her shell-whistle. Selkie pulled herself out of the pool. Fred scrambled up beside her.

'I said the show is over!' the Professor screamed.

'Encore, encore!' the audience screamed back.

Selkie and Fred climbed onto the stage.

Nim blew her whistle again. Selkie dived in, rolling and porpoising round the pool, as if she were loosening up for the swim of her life. Nim dived in and Selkie dived under her so that Nim was riding on her back.

Nim blew the whistle again and Fred dived too, right onto Selkie's back and up to Nim's shoulder.

The audience cheered, the Professor glowered and Nim, Selkie and Fred climbed out of the pool.

The ship slowed down still more.

The Professor moved towards Nim. His eyes were as narrow and glinting as a knife. 'These animals are going back to their cages,' he snarled. 'Get into the elevator.'

Nim, Selkie and Fred walked towards it, very, very slowly.

'Wait!' Erin screamed. 'I want to pat Selkie goodbye!'

'And Fred!'

'We want to pat Selkie!'

'Me too, me too!'

Fred scrambled back to Nim's shoulder as the kids swarmed round them, patting Selkie and hugging Nim. Some of the adults joined in and a few who couldn't get close enough handed Erin money to give to Nim. 'A show like that deserves a tip!' said one soaking-wet woman.

Erin shoved the money into Nim's extra-safe pocket, then whispered something to the little pigtailed girl from the Kids' Klub. The girl ran to the Professor and tagged him on the back. 'Spider!' she shouted.

Then Erin and Nim jumped into the elevator.

As the doors shut Nim saw the mob of kids squeal and surge towards the left-hand rail, with the Professor spluttering and bellowing in the middle of them, locked in as firmly as if in a cage.

Nim pushed the button for the Dolphin Deck, the lowest level with an outside deck. The elevator stopped.

'Ready?' asked Erin.

Nim couldn't speak. She nodded.

Erin burst out of the doors and raced to the left-hand side of the ship. 'The Statue of Liberty!' she screamed. 'Look at all the birds around the Statue of Liberty!'

There weren't many passengers down on this deck and

most had been staring out over the left-hand side at the great green statue. But now everyone turned to watch a flock of brightly coloured birds – parrots, rainbow doves, flamingos, eagles and a toucan, all led by an enormous black frigate bird – soar into the grey sky and wheel around the statue's uplifted torch.

No one looked across. If they had, they might have seen a sea lion and a girl with an iguana on her shoulder slip out of the elevator to the right-hand side of the ship.

Every one of them missed the most spectacular trick of all, the one where Selkie flopped onto a deck chair against the railing and pulled herself into her best ever flipper-stand. They missed seeing Fred climb to her flippers and be launched from his own personal diving board as Selkie dived over the ship's rail and down, down, down into the water of New York Harbour.

And they missed seeing Nim take the biggest breath of her life and jump.

THE WATER WAS as cold as ice-cream. Nim gasped as she sank deep and swirling in the waves of the ship's huge wake, but then Selkie was below her, strong and solid, nudging her up through the murky grey.

Nim spluttered out cold water and breathed in warm air. Fred scrambled onto her shoulder; she settled herself on Selkie's back and wrapped her arms round the sea lion's neck. The ship was already far ahead of them. Selkie could swim faster than most boats could sail, but she had to move slowly with Nim on her back. They still had a long way to go.

To Nim's left was the statue of the enormous green woman with the confused tropical birds circling her torch. Beside her was another small island with square, red-brick buildings. Straight ahead was the huge city-island they were trying to reach: an island covered with shining grey towers as tall as the ship was long. It was as different from Nim's island as any place in the world could be.

'YOU,' ALEX SAID to herself when she woke up, 'are the most mixed-up, muddle-headed, woolly-witted woman in the world.'

Alex agreed.

'You were living in a paradise with people you love and you ran away.'

'It's the worst thing I've ever done,' Alex agreed.

'So what are you going to do about it?'

'Go back,' said Alex. 'Go straight back, say I'm sorry and make things right again.'

'You'll go straight to the airport when you get off the ship?'

Alex thought for a second. 'First I'll go to see Delia.'

HALFWAY ROUND THE world, Jack was fast asleep, stretched out behind a row of chairs on the Isla Grande airport floor. It wasn't much more comfortable than the raft, but Jack didn't want to leave the airport and miss the plane. He didn't want anything to keep him from finding Nim and Alex.

NIM HADN'T THOUGHT there'd be so many boats. There were three ships ahead of the Troppo Tourists, boxy orange ferries, small bright yellow water taxis, sleek yachts and more than a dozen sailboats. Small planes darted overhead and a helicopter whirred so fiercely that Selkie forgot about Nim and dived down deep. Nim and Fred floated off in surprise. Suddenly the waves seemed higher and the current seemed stronger – and Nim was colder and more tired than she'd ever been before.

'Selkie!' she shouted. 'Come back!'

Selkie glided up from below, whuffling apologetically as Nim and Fred slid back on.

The buildings got closer. The closer they got, the bigger they grew. They looked as tall as Fire Mountain and they covered the island so thickly Nim wondered how people could walk in between them.

A motorboat roared by; Selkie swerved out of its way, but two sailboats were following, with a whole fleet of other sailboats chasing them and a yellow water taxi zipping through the middle.

'We've got to get out of here!' Nim said.

Selkie veered to the right, away from the racing sailboats. A little grey-and-white tugboat, with red trim and a fat and friendly shape, was coming that way. No matter which way Selkie veered, the tug kept chugging straight towards them. Its engines were slowing and there was a man standing at the bow waving while two others rushed to unclip the lifebelts.

'Hang on!' the Captain shouted from a loudspeaker in the wheelhouse. 'We're coming!'

Nim and Selkie had been friends since Nim was a baby. They both knew what the other was feeling, and now they both knew that they might never get to shore without help.

'And if they try to put us in jail, we'll just have to escape again!' Nim told Selkie and Fred, trying to sound braver than she felt.

The tug was nearly there. The men tossed out the lifebelts; the youngest man threw off his jacket and shoes and jumped in. Nim slipped off Selkie, Fred slipped off Nim and they all swam towards the boat.

'Over here!' shouted one of the men, running to the tug's low, flat back section. 'Daniel, bring her around to the stern!'

'Right!' the young man shouted as he swam desperately towards Nim. 'Don't worry! I'm coming!'

With Daniel on one side and Selkie on the other, Nim swam to the tug.

The two men on deck threw themselves down, reaching over the side to Nim. She grabbed their arms and they pulled her up on board. Daniel followed.

Nim was coughing, spluttering and shaking, and her teeth were chattering so hard she could barely speak. 'Please get Fred!'

Daniel rushed to the edge, 'There's someone else out there?'

Nim pointed. Fred was riding on top of one of the lifebelts.

'That's Fred?' Daniel asked. He was shivering a bit too. 'I guess he can't hang onto the lifebelt if we pull it in?'

Nim shook her head.

'Well,' said Daniel as he got ready to jump in again, 'I sure hope Fred appreciates this.'

But at that moment, Selkie came up under Fred and tossed him onto the deck. Then, with a mighty leap, she flopped up beside him.

The older man came back from the wheelhouse with a blanket and wrapped it snugly around Nim. 'I take it they're friends of yours?' he asked as Fred scurried to Nim's shoulder and Selkie settled herself protectively behind them.

Nim nodded.

'Okay. Because otherwise that's one lost sea lion, let alone the iguana. So what happened?'

'I fell off a boat,' Nim said, pointing vaguely towards the disappearing sailboats.

'You fell off a boat and nobody noticed?'

Nim nodded, her teeth still chattering.

'Hmm. That's not the whole story, is it?'

'No,' Nim said honestly.

'Well, let's get you warmed up and we'll work out what to do with you. What about some hot chocolate? And Daniel, you're the skinniest – how about finding her one of your spare T-shirts so we can dry her clothes?'

Nim went into the cabin and changed into Daniel's T-shirt. It came down to her knees like a dress, so she could hang her own clothes out over the line to dry in the sun.

'Now,' said the older man, when Nim reappeared. 'Let's start with names. You can call me Ivan, and you are?'

'Nim Rusoe.'

'And where are your parents, Miss Nim Rusoe? Who am I going to call to say we've fished you out of the harbour and could they please come and pick you up?'

'My mum's dead,' said Nim, 'and you can't call my dad. But I'm looking for my friend Alex Rover.'

'Alex Rover, like the author?' asked Ivan.

'Nim, like *Nim's Island*?' asked Daniel, pointing to a water taxi zipping towards the shore. On its side was an enormous poster of a girl with a spyglass at her eye and an iguana on her shoulder, leaning out from the top of a palm tree while a sea lion splashed in the cove below. '*Nim's Island*' was written round the top, and 'the newest by ALEX ROVER' in even bigger letters underneath.

Nim's brain couldn't believe what her eyes were seeing. It was like looking into her rainwater pool and seeing a strange, almost-Nim reflection looking back at her.

'Yes,' she whispered. 'That's me.'

18

JACK CHECKED HIS email at the airport again before his flight left. There was still nothing from Alex or Nim. Before, Jack hadn't known if he was more scared or angry. Now he knew: he was just plain scared. Because it didn't make sense. Alex would never have taken Nim without telling him. And Nim would never have meant to leave without telling him.

But what else could have happened? What if they'd been kidnapped by the supply plane pilot? What if he'd come right across the world to find them and they were still somewhere near the island?

Maybe he should jump straight onto a plane home the instant he landed.

'I've got this far,' he decided. 'I'll look for them in the city first.'

But as the plane roared up the runway, Jack suddenly remembered that if someone's name wasn't in his email address book, the message went into the Trash folder unless it had the words 'science' or 'research' in the subject line. And the Trash folder had blinked every time he'd checked his emails.

Alex and Nim didn't know that.

There could be an email from them in the Trash right now! Jack thought bitterly.

But he'd have to wait till the plane landed before he could check.

IVAN WAS JUST about to phone Delia Defoe to tell her about Nim when a call came in over their radio. A big cruise ship needed a tugboat to tow it up the Hudson River to its dock.

'I guess we could take you with us,' said Ivan. 'Maybe someone could meet you at the cruise ship terminal.'

'No!' Nim exclaimed. 'I can't go anywhere near the cruise ships!'

Ivan looked at her shrewdly. 'You might have to tell us a bit more of your story, young Nim.'

'There's a Professor on the ship. He kidnapped Selkie and he wanted Fred too. He said that was the law because of the Foundation for Intelligent, Unique and Interesting Animals – but Selkie's been my friend since I was three and Fred since he was hatched . . . they can't belong to this Foundation and go to live with people to study them. They just can't.'

'So you jumped overboard to save them?' asked Ivan.

Nim nodded.

Daniel whistled.

'Well,' said Ivan, 'you've got the courage of your convictions, that's for sure. I don't see that we've got any choice but to get you where you're going – sea lion, iguana and all. And until the police have sorted out this Professor and his Foundation we'll help you steer clear of him.'

'We could drop you off somewhere else,' Daniel suggested, 'if someone could meet you.'

Ivan phoned Papyrus Publishing. When he asked to speak to Delia Defoe he was put through to her voicemail, and when he phoned back and tried to explain that he had Nim with him and that she needed to find Alex Rover, he was put through to a special recorded announcement about publicity for Alex Rover's new book. When he tried a third time and explained how urgent it was, he was told that Papyrus Publishing never ever gave out an author's address or phone number.

'I'm afraid you'll simply have to go to the publishing house,' said Ivan. 'We could put you in a cab.'

'I don't think a cab would take Selkie,' Daniel said.

'Selkie can't stay behind!' Nim protested and Selkie barked 'NO!'

'I'll phone my sister-in-law Carla,' said Daniel. 'You'd all fit in her delivery van.'

He picked up his phone. Nim could faintly hear Carla on the other end, 'A sea lion? Are you for real?'

The radio crackled. 'The cruise ship's waiting. Is there a problem?'

Daniel grinned as he put away his phone. 'We're in luck – Carla's down near the water taxi dock right now.'

'Give me five minutes!' Ivan said into the radio. 'We've got an emergency delivery to the water taxi dock.'

'Does Carla like sea lions?' Nim asked anxiously.

'Sure! She's just never met one.'

'And marine iguanas?'

'Who wouldn't love Fred?'

Fred smirked and went on munching the salad Ivan had made him.

Nim's clothes were nearly dry. She took them off the line and changed in the cabin as they pulled into the dock.

Ivan handed her a card when she came back to the wheelhouse. 'You'll be fine with Carla. But this has got my name and phone number – you call me if you've got any problems. Call us if you don't have any problems! We want to hear you got there safe.'

'Thank you,' said Nim. 'And thank you for the sandwich and hot chocolate.' If she ever did get back to the island, she thought, maybe she could take some hot chocolate with her.

'Here's my number too,' said Daniel.

'And thank you for rescuing me,' Nim said.

'Anyone jumps off a ship into New York Harbour to rescue their friends,' said Daniel, 'I'd be proud to rescue them.'

'Just don't make a habit of it!' Ivan warned, giving her a warm hug. 'And don't forget to call us.'

The tug bumped up against the dock. Daniel jumped down and Selkie, Nim and Fred followed.

THEY GOT OFF at a park, with a wide stretch of green grass that ended at a path as smooth and hard as rock, and so crowded that everyone had to move with determination and speed. Nim had never imagined that so many people could fit into the same place at the same time.

While they walked they talked on phones, to each other, to themselves; some used words Nim couldn't understand

and languages she'd never heard. They drank cans of soft drink and cups of coffee, ate ice-cream on sticks and hot dogs and pretzels, carried purses and briefcases and fat bags with shopping or small dogs inside – and somehow they hardly ever bumped into each other.

'Come on,' said Daniel. 'Carla's waiting. It'll be fine.'

Nim took a deep breath. Fred curled himself tighter round her neck. Selkie pressed hard against her. They followed Daniel down the path.

Next to the path was a road and on the road there were cars. Lots of yellow cars and lots of every-other-colour-in-the-world cars. Some were going one way and some were going the other, but just when Nim thought they'd meet *smash* in the middle, they slipped safely on by.

Nim had seen pictures of cars, but she'd never heard the noise or smelled the smell. The smell was hot and the noise was hotter, and just when she thought it couldn't get any louder there was a high-pitched siren, a roaring noise like a sea lion bull and a huge red truck screamed past.

Selkie didn't like this place with all its strange noises and she wanted to get through it as fast as she could. She galumphed off the path onto the road.

Cars honked and brakes screeched.

'Selkie!' shouted Nim, dashing into the road after her.

'Wait!' shouted Daniel, grabbing Nim's arm.

'What part of *DON'T WALK!* don't you understand?' shouted a taxi driver at the people dashing across while the cars stopped for Selkie.

Sellkie barked crossly and flopped back up onto the path.

'It's Nim and the sea lion!' shouted a woman on the opposite side of the street.

'Is that who you're supposed to be?' a man called. 'Are you supposed to be Nim?'

'Great publicity stunt!' cheered another man.

Then the cars stopped and so did the flashing sign of a little red man walking. As everyone stepped onto the road the sign below lit up to show a little white man walking.

So that's how they know when to do it! thought Nim as she stepped up onto the pavement on the other side.

They hurried on through a little park, ignoring the flowers and cool splashing fountain. At the end of the park was an enormous bull.

Selkie barked and wouldn't go on.

'It's okay!' Nim coaxed. 'He's just a statue!'

Selkie froze into her statue trick and the people who were lined up to have their pictures taken with the bull ran over to take pictures of Selkie too.

'Is that a real sea lion?'

'Is it safe?'

'Of course,' said Nim and a woman rushed up to stand beside her while her friend took a picture. Fred reached over and gulped the top off her ice-cream cone.

'Sorry,' said Nim, though Fred wasn't sorry at all.

There was a whisper of excitement and more people kept coming and taking more pictures.

'Got to keep moving, guys!' Daniel said.

'Where are you going?' a long-haired man called.

'Papyrus Publishing.'

'Have you got the address?' asked a grandmotherly woman, writing it on the back of her shopping list. 'My son works there.'

'That's a long way uptown,' said a woman in a red suit. 'How're you going to get them there?'

'You could take the subway!' suggested the long-haired man.

'You can't take a sea lion on the subway!' said the red-suited woman. 'You need to call one of those cabs that takes dogs.'

'My sister uses those to take her dogs to day care,' said a carpenter walking past. 'I'll call her and get their number.'

'Thanks,' said Daniel, 'but we've already got a ride.' They crossed the road to a woman opening the back door of a van covered with pictures of dogs and the sign *Carla's Canine Cakes*.

19

CARLA KISSED DANIEL, hugged Nim, patted Selkie and almost patted Fred, all at once and all while she was talking. 'Glad to help out. I thought Daniel must be kidding, but you're for real all right. You can tell me your story on the way – where is it you need to go?'

Daniel gave her the address, ruffled Nim's hair and jogged back to the dock where the tugboat was waiting.

'We've got a few deliveries to do on the way,' said Carla. 'Cakes can't wait! I've stacked up the boxes so the sea lion can fit – Selkie, is it? – Selkie, can you hop right in there, honey? Just don't squish the boxes!'

Selkie flopped into the back of the van, in front of the stacked cake boxes. It was cool and if she sat up high, she'd be able to see out of the back window. She gave a honk of approval.

'And what about this little guy?' Carla asked, pointing to Fred. 'He's

not going to climb all over
the boxes, is he?'

'He might,' said Nim.

'Okay, Freddy, in the front with
Fritz. And you too, Nim. Fritz, stop
barking, I'm sure Fred's much nicer
than he looks. Buckle up and off we
go; we've got a bunch of cakes to
get where they're going.'

Fritz was a dachshund, a short-legged, long-bodied dog
about the same size and shape as Fred. At first he squeezed
himself against Carla, but then he wiggled up against Nim.
Fred sneezed jealously; Fritz barked in surprise and then
crawled across Nim to the side window so he could stand
and look out, carefully ignoring Fred.

Fred did the same, carefully ignoring Fritz.

A bus went by. It was completely covered by the same
Nim's Island picture as the water taxi.

Carla laughed. 'Would you look at that! How do you
feel about people staring at you all over Manhattan?'

'A bit strange,' said Nim, because it seemed more polite
than saying it made her feel sick.

'So?' asked Carla. 'Spill the story. What's a kid doing
in New York City all on her lonesome? Or another way to
put it, what's a kid doing with a sea lion and an iguana
and their picture on a bus? You know, I see a lot of strange
things driving around this town, but I've never seen
that before. Now, where did I put the address for that

Dalmatian cake? There it is, under your feet, just grab it for me, will you?'

A yellow car with a *Nim's Island* sign on the back blared its horn.

'Hey!' Carla shouted back. 'I've got the real thing in here, so just watch who you're honking.'

Fritz barked in agreement. Fred sneezed.

'Here we are!' Carla exclaimed a few minutes later, turning into a side street and stopping with a jolt. 'We'll have to get Selkie out so I can reach the cake . . . will you guys be okay while I run it up? It's only half a block, twelfth floor, this says – won't take me more than ten minutes.'

'We'll be fine,' said Nim.

But Selkie had seen a pond.

It was a wide, shallow pond in a small park, with a splashing fountain in the middle. Two boys and a girl were standing in the fountain, and a mother and baby were slapping at the shallow water at the pond's edge. Selkie galumphed down the pavement, through a big marble arch and cannonballed in. The pond was even more shallow than she'd realized, and instead of sinking down she skidded right across to the other side.

The baby laughed and clapped his hands. His mother whisked him up and stood ready to run.

'She won't hurt him!' Nim called, jogging across with Fred and Fritz close behind.

'Okay,' said the mum and after a while she put the baby down again to splash and watch.

Selkie rolled on her back and Nim splashed water over her dusty belly. Fred waded across to the fountain. Fritz followed him, until Fred climbed into the jet of spray and was bubbled up and over the edge.

'Cool!' said one of the boys.

'Is he yours?' asked the other.

'And the sea lion?' asked the girl.

'They're my friends,' said Nim.

'Do you belong to a circus?'

'We don't belong to anyone,' said Nim. 'We're just us.'

But now she could see Carla crossing the street back towards the park. 'Fred!' she called, 'Selkie! Fritz! Time to get going!'

The kids ran back to the van with them, waving goodbye as they drove off.

ALEX SAW THE Statue of Liberty out of her cabin window as the ship sailed past. She had nothing to pack but the pyjamas and toothbrush she'd bought and the book that Delia had sent her.

For the first time, she opened her new book and began to read.

The ship slowed to nearly a full stop. The engines were barely purring. There seemed to be quite a long wait before a tugboat towed it to the dock.

Alex began to smile as she read.

The ship docked. Ropes were run out and looped over the bollards on the dock; the gangplank slammed down.

Alex looked up, wishing she were reading the book aloud to Jack and Nim, with Fred, Selkie and Chica looking on.

People were walking past her window, wheeling suitcases and carrying backpacks.

The mother of the next-door children called, 'But I asked you to pack this morning!' and the children shouted, 'We were busy!'

Alex went on reading.

Virginia knocked on the door to tell her it was time to leave the ship and ask if she needed help with her bags.

'No thanks,' said Alex and went to stand in the queue to say goodbye to the crew. It was a long line and she went on reading as she stood.

She shook hands with the Captain and saw that the family in the cabins next door had lined up behind her. The children looked as bouncy and friendly as they'd sounded through the walls, and Alex wished she'd been brave enough to meet them. She joined an even longer line to show her passport and leave the dock – and very nearly finished the book.

'But I do know the ending,' she reminded herself. 'At least, I think I do.'

Suddenly she could hardly wait to get off the ship and sort out the ending to her even newer story.

'DO YOU SEE that woman's book?' Ben asked Erin.

Erin stared hard. She read the title and she felt a bit sick. 'Do you think Nim just read it and made everything up?'

'She couldn't have. She had Fred.'

'And Selkie.'

'It's still very weird.'

'What's even weirder is that woman's wearing trousers like Nim's. *Nobody* has trousers like Nim's.'

'And she hasn't got a suitcase.'

'As if she got on in a hurry . . .'

'. . . like Nim.'

'Do you think it could be?'

'Let's ask her!'

But by the time all their passports were stamped and bags checked, Alex had vanished.

Ben and Erin followed their parents and the twins out to stand in line for a taxi. The first one to pull in had a sign on the roof: *Nim's Island by ALEX ROVER. In stores 14 July!*

'That's today,' said Erin.

'So the only person on the ship who could already be reading it . . .'

'. . . is Alex Rover.'

Ben started to giggle. 'Can you imagine what she'll say when she sees Nim!'

'And Selkie and Fred!'

JACK'S PLANE DIDN'T go all the way to New York; he had to change planes twice. He rushed to check his email again at an airport computer as he waited for the last plane. This time he went straight to the Trash folder. It was crammed with messages.

As he skimmed down the list, his heart started thumping so fast he could hardly breathe.

From: erin@kidmail.com
To: jack.rusoe@explorer.net
Date: Wednesday 14 July, 11:30
Subject: Very very urgent about Nim

Dear Mr Rusoe,

I'm the girl who sent Nim's emails to you before. I hope you don't think I'm rude but I think it's very mean that you haven't written to Nim yet. Anyway, I thought you'd like to know that the ship is in New York now and it's going to dock in about half an hour. We're getting off at the cruise ship terminal but Nim and Selkie and Fred jumped off when everyone was looking at the Statue of Liberty.

'Jumped off the ship?' Jack exclaimed.

Nim didn't ask me to write to you this time but I hope it's okay because she's worried that you're angry at her about Alex. And she's my friend so I don't want her to be upset, so could you please write to her soon. I guess she can check her email when she finds Alex.

From Erin Caritas

Jack felt hot and cold and didn't know if he was going to be sick or explode, or maybe both at the same time. He read the email again even though every word was already burned into his brain, especially 'jumped off the ship' and 'when she finds Alex'.

Then he went down through all the emails that had gone straight into the Trash every time he'd checked for mail from Nim or Alex.

He found all five messages that Nim had asked Erin to write. When he'd finished reading he knew that:

- Nim, Selkie and Fred had jumped off a ship in the middle of New York Harbour about two hours ago.
- They weren't with Alex.

There were lots more things that he didn't know, but the most important were:

- Did Nim, Selkie and Fred drown when they jumped off the ship?
- If they hadn't drowned, where were they now?
- Where was Alex?

The other things he really wanted to know but would worry about later were:

- Why did they get onto the ship?
- How did they get onto the ship?
- When did they get onto the ship?
- Why did Alex leave?

But the most important question of all he couldn't even ask because no one knew the answer:

- Would they all find each other again?

To: erin@kidmail.com
From: jack.rusoe@explorer.net
Date: Wednesday 14 July, 12:01
Subject: Re: Very very urgent about Nim

Dear Erin,

Do you really mean that Nim jumped off a ship and swam to land?

I'm arriving in New York at 18:00 this evening on Flight 123. If you talk to Nim please tell her.

I'm very sorry I didn't read your emails before.

Yours truly,

Jack Rusoe

P.S. Thank you for being Nim's friend.

He started another email.

From: jack.rusoe@explorer.net
To: aka@incognito.net

The airport loudspeaker crackled. 'Passenger Jack Rusoe, please go to Boarding Gate 46 immediately. Your flight is about to leave.'

Jack left the computer and raced to the gate. Five more hours till I'm there, he thought.

It was going to be the longest five hours of his life.

CARLA DROVE NIM and her friends past old buildings, new buildings, buildings of carved stone, buildings of shiny glass and building after building whose tops were high above the clouds. None of them were where Alex's books were published.

How would I ever have found Delia Defoe by myself? Nim wondered. And if I couldn't find her, how would I ever find Alex?

They passed banks, dress shops, camera shops, jewellery shops, postcard shops, toy shops, pet shops, hotels, cafes and stands on the street corners selling handbags or sunglasses or snacks and drinks. They saw flags waving, neon signs flashing, steps going down into the ground and steam hissing up from a hole in the path, the way it did from the Hissing Stones when Fire Mountain was getting angry.

They stopped at traffic lights and watched the people crossing.

'Isn't it funny,' Nim said. 'There are so many people – and none of them are ever the same!'

'That's what makes life interesting, honey,' said Carla.

'But what I want to see is the apartment waiting for this poodle birthday cake . . . don't yap, Fritz, poodles are nice too. Let's see, if I turn here, go down this street and now . . . oh, dear, that was exactly what I didn't want to do. Okay, we'll have to park here and walk. You guys can hop out and stretch if you want, better put Fritz on his leash – does Fred have a leash?'

'He can go on my shoulder,' said Nim.

'Okay, don't go far, I'll be as quick as I can.' Carla opened the back of the van to let Selkie out, grabbed the cake box and raced off. Nim and the others followed more slowly, with Selkie pressed close to Nim's side.

On the corner a man was selling pretzels. The pretzels were like bread twisted into knots and covered with salt. Fred liked salt. He leaned out from Nim's shoulder and chomped half a pretzel from the stand.

'That'll be one dollar!' said the man.

I don't have any money! Nim thought, but then she remembered the tips Erin had dropped into her pocket as they got into the elevator. She showed them to the pretzel seller.

'Too much!' he said, taking one green piece and giving her back the rest. Nim bought a bottle of water too and she still had money left.

They crossed the road, turned the corner – and walked into a solid wall of people. Most of them tried to jump out of Selkie's way, though they were too jammed in to jump far.

The people were staring at giant screens on the fronts

of buildings on both sides of the street. Some of the screens had pictures that changed from one thing to another and back again; others had brightly lit words running across them, starting over again as soon as they'd finished.

One of the running signs said: ALEX ROVER'S *NIM'S ISLAND* RELEASED TODAY.

Nim felt as if the only things that were real were the feel of Fred's spine under her chin and the warmth of Selkie's shoulder.

'Let's get back to the van,' she said, but they were squashed in so tight there was barely room to turn round.

'Whoof!' Selkie barked, 'Whoof-WHOOF!'

The crowd shifted just enough for Nim to get through – but then more people noticed Selkie and Fred and crowded closer to see.

'They're from Alex Rover's new book!'

'No, they must be filming a movie!'

More people crushed closer. A policeman whistled. Selkie stopped, but the whistle wasn't for her. It was to make the cars stop so Selkie and Nim could cross, with their long parade following behind.

'Where are we going?' a girl asked.

'Back to Carla's van,' said Nim. 'And then to find Alex Rover.'

'We're on TV!' shrieked a boy, leaping in front of Nim to wave to a man walking backwards with a camera on his shoulder.

Some people stopped following her then, but others

came closer to ask about Alex. One man pushed his way through with a pen and a book, and asked Nim to sign it. It was Alex's book – and even though looking at it made Nim feel sorry, ashamed and confused, when she read Alex's name, she felt a tiny trickle of hope that maybe Alex would still like her after all.

The man kept on asking till Nim scribbled her name across the face of the girl who was supposed to be her.

'Can I have your autograph too?' a boy asked, but just as other people started pulling out pieces of paper, notebooks and hats, Fred sneezed. Hard.

Everyone stepped back.

Fred looked smug as they met Carla and started off again. The van crawled through the traffic. 'We're nearly there,' Carla explained. 'What we're going to do is loop around, drop off this dog-that-looks-like-a-cat cake – stop yapping, Fritz – though you're right, who'd want a dog that looks like a cat? But this customer does, so that's what they're getting, and then we'll get Nim where she needs to be.'

Carla turned where the road met a wide green park. Nim saw soft grass, flowers, tall trees and hills. It was like the fresh green heart of this hot, busy city.

In the park, people walked and dreamed, lay on the grass, jogged, rollerbladed, rode bikes and horses. There were mothers with babies, fathers with toddlers, grandparents with grandchildren, mothers and fathers with little kids and big kids and almost grown-up kids.

Families! thought Nim and suddenly she didn't want to see any more.

CARLA PARKED IN a row of horses and carriages in front of a palace. It looked like a picture in a book Nim had at home. 'Don't go away!' Carla said, letting them all out again to get the dog-that-looked-like-a-cat cake. 'I'll just be a minute!'

Selkie honked in surprise at the horses. She'd never seen animals with such long legs. A big grey horse whinnied back and Selkie lolloped over to meet it.

'You're a long way from home!' the driver said to Selkie. 'It's a good thing Mabel likes tourists.' He rubbed the horse's neck affectionately.

Mabel and Selkie sniffed noses. Fred and Fritz gulped some popcorn they'd found on the ground.

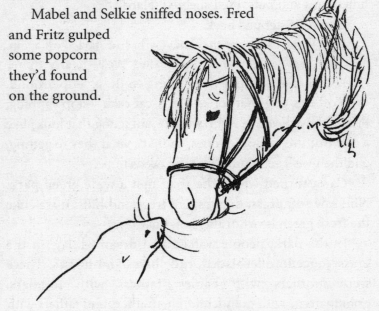

Nim was the only one who couldn't enjoy the horses and carriages, the golden fountain or the palace, the brilliant sunshine or the green park. Because soon she'd be at Alex's publisher, and if Delia Defoe couldn't help her, she had no idea at all what she was going to do next.

Carla bustled back, looking flushed and cross. 'Turns out they wanted two cakes! Would have been nice if they'd told me when they ordered! So I'm thinking . . . do you want to go back to the shop with me and then I can go in to find this Delia with you?'

But Nim couldn't wait any longer. 'We can go in by ourselves,' she said, though she was suddenly more afraid than she'd been ever since she stood at the railing to dive off the ship.

'Okay then . . . but don't think I'm dumping you off for good. I'll just be about an hour – plenty of time to sort out if this Delia gal can help you. Then I'll come back and see what's happening, and you can all come and stay with me till you find your friend or your dad or whoever.'

'We can stay with you?' Nim asked, amazed.

'Well, I'm hardly going to let you sleep out in Central Park! For one thing Daniel would never speak to me again. Though I warn you, at my house it'll be a squish.'

Nim tried to say thank you, but her throat was even more choked now than when she'd been afraid.

'Here we are!' Carla pulled up in front of a tall, shining building with Alex Rover's name hung in a banner across a window display of *Nim's Island* books. She gave Nim a card, hugged her hard and patted Fred before opening the back door for Selkie. 'Here's my number in case you need it. Remember I'll be back in a hour.'

She pulled back into the traffic, sticking her head out the window to shout once more, 'Don't worry!'

'I won't,' Nim lied as she waved goodbye.

She pushed the door.

It was a heavy glass door, and when Nim stepped in, another door followed close behind, so there was only just enough space for Nim and Fred. Selkie threw herself at the second door so hard that all the doors spun around and Nim ended up back on the street where she'd begun.

She tried again. This time she got into the building and so did Selkie.

Books in glass cases were on every side, up to the ceiling. Nim knew she was in the right place.

Three men were sitting behind a desk.

'Oh, my goodness!' said the first.

'You'd think publicity could have told us!' said the second.

'Let me guess,' said the third. 'You must be Nim!'

'Yes,' said Nim, 'I need to see Alex Rover.'

The men looked at each other.

'Get Delia Defoe,' said one and the second man picked up the phone.

'Wait there, sweetie,' said the third and Nim and Selkie sat down in front of the bookcases. Nim read the titles while Fred stretched out under the shelf. Selkie watched the people coming in and going out through the heavy revolving door.

Elevator doors opened and a woman stepped out.

'I'm Alex Rover's editor,' she said. 'I appreciate your interest in this book and I'm very intrigued about how you organized these animals so fast, but Alex Rover doesn't give interviews.'

'I don't want an interview,' said Nim. 'I just have to talk to her.'

'Most people think Alex Rover's a man – why do you think she's a woman?'

'Because she's my friend,' said Nim. 'At least, she was.'

'Well, I could give her your message: why do you need to see her?'

'To say I'm sorry,' Nim muttered, hiding her face against her knees so Delia wouldn't see her cry.

'Do you mean,' Delia said softly, as if she couldn't quite believe what she was asking, 'that you're the real Nim? And this is truly Fred – and Selkie?'

Nim nodded.

Delia squatted down on the floor beside her and Nim told her the story; everything except exactly what she'd said to Alex, because she thought Delia wouldn't want to help her if she knew just how horrible Nim had been.

At first Delia looked excited, but as the story went on she looked more and more concerned.

'So now can you tell me how to find Alex?' asked Nim.

'I'd love to,' said Delia. 'The problem is – I don't have any idea.'

21

WHEN ALEX FINALLY got out of the cruise ship terminal, she could see the top of the Papyrus Publishing building, tall and shining above the others around it. There was a long queue for taxis and Alex needed to get there fast. She crossed the road and started to walk.

She wrote her email to Nim and Jack in her head as she walked. It wasn't easy, but she knew what she had to say. The only thing she didn't know was what their answer would be.

She was thinking about them so hard that sometimes she'd see a girl with hair like Nim's, or a man who walked like Jack, and for half a moment she'd think, They're here!

It was so bad that when she looked in the window of her publisher's building, she thought she saw Selkie sitting in front of the bookcases.

'You,' Alex told herself, 'are going absolutely fruitcake nutty!'

'But,' she added, 'in five more minutes you can email them.'

'FIRST THINGS FIRST,' Delia was saying to Nim. 'Come up to my office to email Alex and your father – Selkie and Fred can stay down here, can't they?'

Selkie barked and pressed hard against Nim, while Fred scrambled up to her shoulder.

'Okay,' said Delia. 'I guess we can take the goods elevator.'

Suddenly Selkie barked louder and skidded across to the revolving door as fast as she could lollop.

'Selkie!' shouted Nim.

And then she saw Alex.

They raced across the floor and met in the middle, hanging on just as tight as they had when Nim had pulled Alex out of her sinking sailboat. Selkie whuffled around them in a loving circle and Fred climbed up to Alex's shoulder.

'But how?' Alex asked. 'And when?'

'On a ship,' said Nim. 'I'm sorry, I'm so sorry.'

'Where's Jack?'

'I think he's very mad at me. I don't know why I said such terrible things.'

'Do you mean you came *alone*?'

'That's what she means,' said Delia. 'Which is one of the many reasons I'm so happy to see my best-selling author!'

Alex let go of Nim for just long enough to shake Delia's hand. 'Before we do anything else,' she said, 'could we please email Jack?'

Delia led them round to the goods elevator and they all rode up to Delia's office, with Nim and Alex still both talking at once and trying to explain.

'. . . and then we jumped off,' said Nim. 'Near the green lady.'

'Jumped off what?' asked Alex, feeling sick.

'The ship,' said Nim.

Alex felt even sicker. 'What ship?' she asked when she could breathe again.

Nim told her and Alex told Nim her story, and Nim laughed and cried and Alex cried and laughed, when they realized that Nim had been hiding in a lifeboat right outside Alex's cabin for that whole week.

Then Alex checked her email and the messages came flooding in. She read through Jack's messages from the last right back to the first. The more she read the paler she got, because Jack was so angry and sad she knew he'd never want to see her again.

'But I told him what happened,' Nim said sadly. 'Erin sent an email every day.'

'Maybe he was too sad to understand,' said Alex.

From: aka@incognito.net
To: jack.rusoe@explorer.com
Date: Wednesday 14 July, 14:02
Subject: I've found Alex!

Dear Jack,

You shouldn't be angry at Alex because it's not her fault that I left. But it's **my** fault **she** left.

I wish you could come too.

We are going down to the sea now so Selkie and Fred can swim in salt water, because they've just been in fountains today. I hope your email is working so you get this and I hope you answer.

Love (as much as Selkie loves us),

Nim

'But what if the Professor tries to catch Selkie again?' Nim asked.

'NO ONE is ever going to take Selkie away again!' said Alex. She looked so fierce that Nim believed her.

DELIA'S PHONE RANG. 'There's someone waiting for you downstairs,' she said and for just a minute both Nim and Alex thought, Jack!

They all rode the goods elevator back down to the lobby, and though it wasn't Jack, Nim was still very glad to see Carla. Fred was glad to see Fritz, and Alex and Delia were glad to meet someone who'd helped Nim. There were more thank yous, more exclaiming and explaining and then Carla and Fritz dashed off to start baking tomorrow's cakes.

A long white car with black windows pulled up in front. The driver got out to open the doors.

'Here's your car,' said Delia. 'Are you sure you don't want me to organize a hotel?'

'Thanks,' said Alex, 'but I'd like to do it myself. It's time I learned to do things like that.'

A boy and a girl with their mother stopped to stare as Alex, Delia, Nim and Fred, and finally Selkie, came out through the revolving doors.

'Look at the sea lion!'

'That kid's got a lizard on her shoulder!'

'Oh, they're just advertising a book,' said the mother.

Nim and Alex looked at each other and laughed so hard they had to lean against the limousine before they could get into it.

Delia waved goodbye as the car pulled out, with Nim and Alex sitting beside each other, Fred on the back of the seat staring out of a window and Selkie sitting on the floor and staring out of hers.

Alex pushed a button in the limousine's door and her window rolled down. Nim pushed the button for Selkie, but rolled Fred's down just enough that he could put his head out and not so far he could fall out by mistake.

'Help yourself to a drink,' the driver said.

There were bottles in a cupboard behind the driver's seat. Nim had to pour the water into a lid for Fred. Selkie could drink hers from the bottle.

The limousine driver politely asked Selkie not to put her head out of the window with the bottle in her mouth. Selkie finished her water fast: she liked having her head out of the window.

When they stopped at a light, three dogs crossed the road in front of them.

'WHOOF!' honked Selkie, racing from one window to the next.

'Arf!' the dogs yipped in surprise.

Selkie whuffled happily. Limousines were much nicer than being on her own in the back of a van, trying not to move in case she squashed cakes.

THE DRIVER TOOK them to another park a little further up the river from where the tugboat had brought Nim that morning. There was a marina with boats moored all along the wharves: sailboats, motorboats and some that looked more like floating houses. One had flower boxes at its windows and a 'For Rent' sign on its bow.

'Interesting!' Alex said thoughtfully. 'But I'm starving. Let's get something to eat.'

Fred rubbed his spiky back against her ankle. He'd nearly forgotten how much he liked Alex.

The four of them walked together across the green grass to a cafe in the middle. They sat at an outside table, where Selkie and Fred could watch the dogs sitting at other tables with their people. Alex ordered fish and chips and salad, but added, 'One fish needs to be raw, please!'

'Of course!' said the waiter and brought Selkie and Fred a bowl of water to share while they waited.

'I didn't know you had sea lions in New York City,' said the man at the next table.

'We're just visiting,' Alex explained.

'And I love your mother-and-daughter outfits!' his wife exclaimed. 'Did you make them yourself?'

Alex looked embarrassed. 'We're not . . .'

'Yes,' said Nim.

Alex's eyes filled up with tears. 'We'll have to find somewhere to check emails after dinner,' she said – because even though Nim had forgiven her for leaving, she didn't know if Jack ever could.

'But Selkie and Fred need to swim first,' said Nim and so when they'd finished, they wandered down to the marina. Fred and Selkie lolloped across the park and into the water – and as they ran, more and more people came to stare.

'Quick!' said Alex and they raced to the end of a pier where a sign said: 'Kayaks for hire'.

'Have you kayaked before?' the woman asked.

'Of course!' said Alex.

They climbed in and started to paddle. They were splashing as much water as Selkie in a fountain, but somehow they didn't move very far or very fast.

'Are you sure you've done this before?' Nim asked.

'It might have been in one of my books,' said Alex. 'I get mixed up.'

ERIN AND BEN were at the airport with their family, waiting for the plane to take them the rest of the way home. They were early, the plane was late and they were bored with waiting. Erin wanted to check her email, but there were no computers to do it.

'What's so important it can't wait till we get home?' her dad teased.

Erin thought maybe it was time to tell him. 'It's about Nim,' she began.

'She's on TV!' shouted Ben.

'Amazing scenes in New York earlier today,' said the television news above their heads, 'when Times Square played host to a visiting sea lion.'

Erin spun round to see Nim, Selkie and Fred pushing through crowds in the square with the giant computer screens.

'Originally thought to be a publicity stunt for today's release of Alex Rover's new book *Nim's Island* . . .'

The camera showed a *Nim's Island* bus.

'. . . events have now taken a dramatic turn, with a

spokesman for the Troppo Tourist Cruise Ship claiming that this girl . . .' Nim's face filled the screen '. . . had in fact stowed away and stolen the highly trained, valuable sea lion from their care.'

'Liar!' shouted Ben.

'NIM!' shouted a man standing beside them. He was staring up at the screen with shock, relief and rage all dancing over his face – and he had bright eyes and baggy red trousers.

'You're Nim's dad!' shouted Erin.

'Who's Nim?' asked the twins.

The television showed Selkie porpoising around Nim and Alex's kayak.

'Our friend!' Erin and Ben said together.

'You're Erin?' exclaimed Jack.

'And Ben,' said Ben.

'Tell me everything!' said Jack.

The camera showed the Professor pointing accusingly. It narrowed in on the tranquillizer gun at his side.

'That's the man who seal-napped Selkie!'

'And the other animals and birds.'

'Nim didn't mean to stow away – she was trying to rescue Selkie!'

'We've got to help!'

'Police have been called to recapture the animal,' said the reporter.

Jack ran towards the Exit sign.

'Wait!' shouted Mr Caritas. 'I'll come with you!'

'We all will,' said Mrs Caritas.

They raced together through the airport to the long line of yellow taxis parked outside. Jack jumped into the first one with Erin, Ben and their dad and Mrs Caritas and the twins grabbed the one behind.

'This is an emergency,' said Jack. 'To the kayak pier – as fast as you can!'

'The one on the news?' asked the driver. 'With the sea lion?'

'Yes. Please hurry!'

'Gotcha!' said the driver and pulled out so fast they were knocked back in their seats.

The taxi zigzagged and zipped between lanes. Jack closed his eyes so he didn't have to see the scenery blurring past and listened hard to Erin and Ben telling him what had happened on the ship. His face was white; sometimes he looked angry and sometimes he groaned – but sometimes he smiled.

'Nim's never had a kid friend before,' he said at last. 'She's very lucky to have met you two.'

'We like her,' said Erin.

'We've never met anyone like her,' said Ben.

'I can believe that,' said Jack.

They told him about seeing Alex in the morning and his face grew even paler and sadder, and he didn't say anything at all.

'Why didn't you tell your mum and me about this before?' Mr Caritas asked.

'We were afraid . . .'

'Because the Professor said he'd put Nim in jail!'

'That's not going to happen!' their father and Jack said together.

They crossed a bridge to reach the city. The taxi honked and blared its way through the traffic and down to the pier. They could see the masts of sailboats and a crowd of people gathered on the shore.

Jack handed a wad of money to the driver, leaped from the cab and ran.

A policeman stopped him. 'Whoa! Stop right there. We've got a wild animal loose.'

'But that's my daughter!' said Jack. 'The girl, not the sea lion. The sea lion's her friend. They've grown up together.'

'And the woman?'

'She's . . .' said Jack. 'Well, she used to be . . . I mean, I know who she is but I don't know if . . .'

'I see,' said the policeman. 'But the gentleman over there informs me that the animal is extremely dangerous if approached by untrained people, so I can't let you past.'

'That *gentleman*,' said Jack, his face turning scarlet with fury, 'is a wildlife poacher. Search his ship and you'll find other animals that need to be rescued. *He's* the only dangerous animal here.'

The Professor hadn't noticed Jack. He strode over to the policeman. 'We can't wait any longer – that animal needs to be got back into captivity. I'll shoot it with a tranquillizer dart.'

'You're not going to tranquillize that sea lion!' said Jack.

'Everybody keep calm!' said the policeman to the Professor. Because Erin and Ben, their mother and father and the twins had sneaked behind the crowd to where the kayaks were kept. They were now paddling in tight circles around Selkie.

More people from the crowd followed, until every kayak on the pier was surrounding Selkie, blocking her from the Professor.

A reporter pushed his way up to the policeman, followed by a man in a chauffeur's uniform. 'This man says he drove the sea lion down here in his limousine and it wasn't dangerous at all.'

'I'll second that!' said Carla, racing across the lawn with Fritz at her heels. 'She doesn't even squash cakes!'

'I don't know if she belongs to anyone,' said Daniel, 'but I know she loves that little girl and that Nim loves her.'

'And I think you'll find,' said Ivan, 'that this is the wildlife poacher I reported to the police earlier today.'

'What do you say to all that?' the reporter demanded, shoving his microphone in the Professor's face.

'I say I'm getting that animal back!' shouted the Professor.

'Put the gun down!' shouted the policeman.

The Professor ignored him and raised his dart gun.

Jack sprang at him.

The policeman sprang too.

Jack and the policeman clunked heads and their heads clunked the Professor's arm.

'Ow!' screamed the Professor as the tranquillizer dart jabbed his leg. 'Ooh,' he moaned as the injection went in. He slumped down and was asleep before the policeman's handcuffs clamped round his arm.

Jack ran across the grass faster than he'd ever run. He dived into the water and swam straight out. Selkie honked her happiest honk as she dived towards him.

'Jack!' Nim shouted.

'Jack!' Alex whispered.

They reached for him – and their kayak tipped over.

The three of them clung to the upside-down kayak, laughing and hugging, exclaiming and explaining, till Fred poked his face up between them and Selkie honked anxiously that they needed to get back to shore.

'You're right, Selkie,' said Jack. 'I think it's time for us all to go home.'

'All of us?' asked Nim.

'All of us,' said Alex.

THERE WERE TOO many things to organize to go back to the island right away. 'Besides,' said Nim, 'there's a lot to see in the city!'

So while Jack and Nim went to talk to the police about the Professor, Alex went to see the boat that looked like a cottage and rented it for two weeks. Selkie and Fred liked it because they could get on and off into the river any time they wanted and stay home by themselves when Nim, Jack and Alex did things they didn't want to do. Nim, Jack and Alex liked it because when they got back from a busy day in the busy city they could breathe the fresh air and sit peacefully to watch the sun setting over the river.

They went to museums and saw dinosaurs and tiny fossils, Egyptian mummies and suits of armour, enormous paintings and miniature carvings. They went to a library with paintings on the ceilings and stone lions outside the doors. They walked through the hot city streets and into chilled stores where they bought shoes and clothes, and where women sprayed perfume that made Jack sneeze. They went to a cinema and forgot to eat their popcorn, because the screen was so big and the sound so all around them that they felt as if they were in the story too. They ate bagels and hot dogs and foods Nim had never heard of; they had afternoon tea at the hotel that looked like a palace and rode through the streets in the carriage behind the horse called Mabel. They had a party with all their friends and an iguana-shaped cake that made Fred sneeze with surprise.

But best of all was the hot, hot day they all went to the huge park in the middle of the city. The taxi drove down a gently curving road and dropped them off where a path led to a tranquil green lake. When the driver opened the door, Selkie galumphed halfway down the path before he could even say, 'Here we are!'

'I didn't know sea lions could move so fast!' said the driver. 'Or *him*.'

Fred was racing behind Selkie as fast as his short iguana legs would carry him.

People jumped off the path out of their way, dogs barked and Selkie and Fred slid into the water.

A row of turtles sunning on a log slowly turned their heads to stare, and one by one, disappeared under the water.

Fred came up from the bottom with a grin full of water plants.

Selkie popped up halfway across the lake to check if she could still see Nim. A goldfish tail stuck out of the side of her mouth.

Then one dog after another jumped in and paddled

after Selkie and Fred, splashing and barking in the craziest, splashingest game of coconut-football-without-a-coconut that ever was.

Their families laughed as they watched them.

Other families wandering through the park came to watch too.

And Nim, Alex and Jack watched and laughed too, and sat on the bank together for the rest of the afternoon.

P.S.

From: nim@kidmail.com
To: erin@kidmail.com, ben@kidmail.com
Date: Thursday 29 July, 10:05
Subject: Home on the island

Dear Erin and Ben,

I told you I'd write again as soon as we got back to the island. The city was fun but I'm really happy I'm home now.

Our trip back was very different. This captain let Selkie and Fred have their own pool and I slept in a cabin. It was a lot more comfortable, but I missed doing things with you. Once we saw a whale spouting and I wished you could have seen it too. We stopped at different places to take the smuggled animals back to their homes.

We bought a new sailboat when we got to Sunshine Island so we could sail the rest of the way. Jack was going to build our new boat but Alex said this was a present from her book, and Jack said okay because he wanted us all to be home again as fast as possible.

173

Selkie swam most of the way, which was good because she took up all the deck when she had a nap, and also she liked showing the dolphins around, because they decided to follow us home. So did some of the birds.

Jack says the Professor and the Troppo Captain should stay in jail a long, long time. I hope so. So do Kylie, Kelvin and Kristie. They visited us at the houseboat and said how upset they felt when they found out about the animal smuggling. They're going to work on another boat now and Virginia is going to work in a zoo to help the animals who need to learn how to be free after being in cages for too long.

Did you see I have my own email address now so you can write to me as much as you want. But the best thing is that Jack and Alex said I can invite you to come and stay with us on the island next summer. I hope you'll come.

Love (as much as Selkie loves Fred),
Nim

Turn over to find out how
Nim met Alex Rover, in
an extract from her first
brilliant adventure:

NIM'S
ISLAND

WHEN THE SUN rose pink over Fire Mountain, Nim phoned Jack again, but there was still no answer; no ring; nothing at all.

Nim checked the phone . . . the satellite dish . . . the connections between the solar panel and the phone's battery charger . . .

But everything looked the way it should.

She checked her email, even though she knew he didn't have a computer on his boat.

From: aka@incognito.net
To: jack.rusoe@explorer.net
Date: Tuesday 30 March, 22:21

Dear Jack Rusoe,

Your article 'The Life Cycle of the Coconut Palm' was as fascinating as a feature film and as fact-filled as a documentary! But I still have a couple of questions . . .

1) How long do coconuts float?

2) Do they float well enough to make a raft?

3) How could I build one?

Thank you, Alex Rover

'A letter!' said Nim.

She knew it wasn't hers; she knew that Alex Rover was just asking Jack a science question – but it was still a letter. It was as if someone, somewhere in the world, knew she was alone and was saying hello.

From: jack.rusoe@explorer.net
To: aka@incognito.net
Date: Wednesday 31 March, 6:45

Dear Alex Rover,
    Jack is busy doing science. I hope he will answer your questions tomorrow or maybe the day after.
    From Nim

She had heaps to do and that was good, because she didn't want time to worry about Jack.

She made banana-and-coconut mush and snuggled warmly with Selkie to eat it for breakfast. Fred always forgot that he didn't like bananas, so he snitched a bit from her bowl and spat it out across the rock.

'Yuck, Fred!' said Nim. She didn't feel much like eating now, either.

She watered her garden with bamboo pipes trickling coolly from the pool. She towed wagonloads of seaweed to spread round the plants. She picked ten ripe strawberries and a handful of peas.

Jack loved strawberries.

She
made a
new broom
with a fallen-
down palm branch and
swept the hut again.
She filled in Jack's charts with a big
NO across the space for rain, and the
numbers for barometric pressure and sea
temperature, and EAST for where the wind
was coming from. She wished it would turn
around and blow Jack home, and she climbed
the tall palm tree just in case she could see
the white sails.
And when she couldn't, her stomach tied itself
into a hard, tight knot and she went on being busy.
She mixed up dough to make some bread.
It grew swollen and puffy and she punched it
hard in the middle, oofing the air out of the
puffiness and the knot out of her. She punched
and rolled it, over and over, till her arms were
floppy and the dough-ball was smooth.
Then she wrapped it in a fresh banana leaf and carried
it to the Hissing Stones, where Fire Mountain met the
rocks of Keyhole Cove and fountains of steamy water
sometimes shot high and wild into the air.

Today there was just the small yellow pool splattering slimy bubbles, and the rocks around, too hot to touch, hissing steam from every crack. And the smell, like a rotten frigate bird's egg smashed on the beach.

Nim squatted at the edge, out of the way of the wind and stink. She shaped her dough into eight flat pancakes and flicked them one by one onto the hot rock.

What Nim liked best about cooking bread was watching the dough she'd mixed from dry flour, yeast and water puff into warm, fresh bread. 'Science,' Jack said, but Nim thought it was magic.

Today it was nothing.

Today, when the bread bubbled and puffed in the middle, it didn't even make her smile. When she flipped it over with her bamboo flipping stick and then neatly back into her banana leaf, it was just bread, because cooking bread was what she had to do today. And if she did everything that she was supposed to, then Jack would come home tonight and everything would be all right.

So she went on doing jobs, busy busy busy all day. She heaped fallen branches into a bonfire; beach-combed from the Black Rocks of Keyhole Cove to Shell Beach in front of the hut, and then from the sands of Turtle Beach right to the Frigate Bird Cliffs at the end. (And she found three giant seeds shaped like hearts, ten new sea-shells and half a wooden paddle that made her think, Oh, no! But it wasn't Jack's.)

Suddenly she was too tired to do anything more. She made a banana sandwich and curled up on the rock between Selkie and Fred to read the last chapter of her book.

When she finished, she felt happy and sad at the same time, because the ending was warm and smiley, but she didn't want to say goodbye to the people in the book.

'I'll read it again!' Nim decided and read the title out loud, as if she'd never seen it before: '*Mountain Madness*, by Alex Rover.'

'Alex Rover!' she shouted.

Fred fell off the rock and Selkie honked crossly at being woken from her nap. 'Sorry,' said Nim.

She opened the book again and unfolded the newspaper bookmark.

ALEX ROVER – AUTHOR OR HERO?

The most famous writer in the world has written a new book: Mountain Madness *(Papyrus Publishing, £7.99).*

Cliff-hanging adventure; romantic love story – read it and you'll think you're living it! You'll feel the cold rush of wind as you jump out of a plane; the sweat on your palms as you abseil down a cliff.

So is Alex Rover the author – or the Hero?

He couldn't describe these adventures if he hadn't lived them. But Alex Rover is not a typical macho action-man.

Anyone lucky enough to meet him will find a very special human being – a mountain climber who finds poetry on the peak; an explorer who sings the glories of the stars.

Unfortunately, meeting him is not easy to do. He refuses

to give interviews or photographs. Delia Defoe, his editor at Papyrus Publishing, claims that she has never met him — or even spoken to him on the phone!

'We correspond by email,' she says.

'We correspond by email,' Nim repeated. It sounded important and funny. 'I correspond with Alex Rover by email.'

'Selkie,' she said, 'Alex Rover's a Hero.'

'Fred,' she added, 'I *correspond* with a Hero.'

Selkie and Fred looked confused. They liked it when Nim used words they knew, like *coconut* and *fish*, *swimming* and *Keyhole Cove*.

But Nim was happy. If Alex Rover could survive all those wonderful adventures, so could Jack. He'd be home tomorrow, just like he said.

From: jack.rusoe@explorer.net
To: aka@incognito.net
Date: Wednesday 31 March, 18:27

Dear Alex Rover,

Jack is still away but I hope he'll be home soon. I'm glad you're a Hero because *Mountain Madness* is the best book I've ever read. It's like real life except more exciting and everyone is so brave. And because it has a happy ending when the Hero and the lady find each other and fall in love.

From Nim

Dear Nim,

Aren't time differences funny? When it's night-time where I live, the sun's coming up for you. You're living in my tomorrow!

The other funny thought is me being a Hero – I'm as un-Hero as anyone can be!

I can climb mountains if they're made out of paper, and swim rivers if they're in my bathtub (with lots of bubble bath) . . .

I'm not even brave enough to talk to reporters. That's why they make up stories about me – one reporter even made up my name and called me Alexander!!

Yours, Alex (Alexandra!) Rover

Nim had never heard the name Alexandra.

Alex Rover had never thought that anyone could be all alone on a tiny island in the middle of the ocean.

And so Nim went on thinking that Alex Rover was a man, and Alex went on thinking that Nim was a girl at home with her mother and maybe brothers and sisters, cousins and friends. And they both thought that they understood each other perfectly.

FAR, FAR OUT in the ocean, a sailboat drifted. On its deck, a man lay sprawled like a boxer who'd lost a fight.

A frigate bird, his dark wings as wide as the man was tall, swooped curiously.

Jack opened his eyes. He was hot, thirsty and sore all over. When he scratched his beard, his hand came back rusty with dry blood.

He sat up and remembered.

He'd been sitting on the deck, watching the plankton glow on the night-time waves. Suddenly a storm had come roaring and he'd pulled down the sails, but the wind didn't care. It threw the boat sideways and he'd reached for the satellite dish as it smashed to the deck.

Now there was a cut on his head and the satellite dish was gone. And if the satellite dish was gone, his phone wouldn't work and he must go home to Nim.

Jack's head hurt and his legs wobbled, but he staggered to the tiller. He pushed the tiller and then he pulled it, but it swung loose and empty in his hand and he knew his rudder was broken. If his rudder was broken, then he couldn't steer.

And if he couldn't steer, his boat was just a big piece of driftwood.